a comedy of nobodies

a comedy of nobodies

A Collection of Stories

Baron Ryan

BLACK
STONE
PUBLISHING

Printed in the United States of America

First edition: 2024
ISBN 979-8-212-23534-1
Fiction / Short Stories (single author)

Version 1

Blackstone Publishing
31 Mistletoe Rd.
Ashland, OR 97520

www.BlackstonePublishing.com

Thank you, Katrina, for everything.

Table of Contents

how to fall in love in 36 questions

(september)

I was once in love with a wise woman who had no idea how I felt about her, and on days when my vain melancholy gets the best of me, I'm reminded of her words: "Good days or bad days, you're living the rented life. All anxieties of the future or hunger for the past, people you fell in love with, phone calls about your car's extended warranty—they have expiration dates. You come here to be a part of what was always there, and when you leave, what was there will still be there, as you left it." I don't know what happened to her, but she taught me to observe gently with aggressive curiosity and nonjudgmental eyes. As a result, I've learned with knowing naivety that the world so far is refreshingly small, and we are refreshingly unoriginal inhabitants. Our pain is plagiarized from the same sources.

I'm walking down Bow Street with my friends Mike and Ted after a café gig. We played classics from the Bee Gees in another of our vain attempts to jazzify songs that never deserved to go near a bass, guitar, and sax trio. We are casualties of the sad irony that jazz is the most inclusive and exclusive clique to belong to.

Ted, our guitar player, has something to say: "They liked us. I could feel it in my tailbone."

"They gave no indication they liked us," Mike (stand-up bass) says. "Actually, I got the distinct sense they despised us."

"Right, but they despised us much less than any other crowd we've played, so, comparatively, they liked us."

With me and Mike, it's all laughs and observations. We communicate mainly through quips, with the goal of one-upping the other's bit each time. Occasionally, though, we allow each other a window of sensitivity, usually after a romantic rejection of some kind, when we can talk openly about the burdens of the messy male psyche. With Ted, forget it. He refuses to feel a thing, the kind of guy who wears plate armor made of pure sarcasm for any human interaction.

We head to a shop called Insomnia Cookies on Bow Street, open all hours of the bare but lingering Harvard nightlife. It is a narrow building that overlooks—and technically lives under—the picturesque Lowell House. Just a glance to the left is the Harvard Lampoon which I only now realize looks like Otto von Bismarck disguised as a building. We arrive at Insomnia Cookies around 8:00 p.m. for a bottle of milk and to meet our fourth musketeer, Nora. Nora comes from an old-moneyed family of rubber-nipple tycoons in Montreal. They supply rubber nipples to every baby and pervert in North America. The four of us, all going into our sophomore year at Harvard, stick together for safety. After our disastrous jazz gig, I glare out the window at the neo-Georgian architecture of Lowell House, slurping milk, mad at myself for everything I didn't do before nineteen. Nora is late to meet us.

The psychology class I enrolled in with Mike, Ted, and Nora isn't going too hot either. We apparently got approval for a group project that Mike, Ted, and I have no awareness of. The way group projects go, it'll be skippered by one person, and that person is Nora. She wrote the pitch and obtained all the permissions, and now we're supposed to conduct some experiment tomorrow morning.

Nora enters Insomnia Cookies in a yellow raincoat, and moments later it starts sprinkling outside. A blue binder is clutched under her arm, like a mother hen's eggs.

"So, what's happening tomorrow?" Mike asks her with gum in his teeth.

Nora blinks. "Did you read my emails about it?"

"I think they ended up in my spam . . ."

"I mean, I did, but can you sort of summarize, or . . ." I say.

Her nostrils twitch. "None of you have any idea what's happening tomorrow, do you?"

Mike and Ted grumble something about how distracted they've been about some vague news in the Middle East.

"It's an experiment," she says.

"What are we experimenting?" I mumble.

The sprinkling outside turns heavier, and fat raindrops percussively thump the window.

Nora scans the room for spies and whispers, "How to fall in love with anyone."

I turn to Mike and Ted for permission to laugh, but they seem more curious than amused.

Nora apparently read studies on increasing the speed of intimacy between strangers. She wants to throw people in rooms without air-conditioning and have them ask each other thirty-six invasive questions that will make the schmucks fall in love.

"What do you mean *anyone*?" Mike asks. "Sounds like voodoo."

"That's the experiment, that's the whole thing." Nora's Quebecois accent gets even heavier when she's riled up. "I want to see if any stranger, no matter how incompatible, can fall in love with anyone who asks them these questions." She thumps her blue binder.

"I have so many questions about these questions," I say.

"Then you should have brought them up before

everything was arranged," she says. "I've booked three hours at William James Hall for us to conduct this experiment tomorrow. Sixteen people volunteered as test subjects. Strangers. All single. I think."

"Where did you find these strangers?" I ask.

"Match.com."

My disastrous semester consists of four courses, including an anthropology course: History of Agnosticism. I have a bad habit of leaving things to the last minute, and like some proverbial joke, I must pay the price by enrolling in courses that aren't full—one of them being History of Agnosticism. The TA dislikes me because she thinks I'm a Mormon, for some reason. I explicitly clarified that I am not Mormon, and she asked if I had a problem with being Mormon. I said no. Then she asked if I had a problem with the Church of Latter-Day Saints in general, and I said no, and that was probably the wrong answer. I should've had objections with every religion, because she replied, "How interesting . . ."

I get a C-minus on my first homework assignment from that anti-Mormon Nazi. After class, I get a message from Nora: *WHERE ARE YOU???*

Oh right, the love study.

I feel a nervous buildup, a feeling I try not to feel and then feel more as a result. I don't know what I'm afraid of.

I go to CVS and pat on some "Sample Only" cologne. It smells like old hand sanitizer after ten minutes on my skin.

The Old Yard flows with students coming out of class. A labyrinth of pathways cuts across the grass, giving the illusion of a pattern or a well-planned route. No sidewalk in Harvard Yard curves—all are sharp, straight, tapered.

I get to William James Hall, the psychology building, passing the modern metallic Science Center and the Gothic Annenberg dining hall. These two buildings provide instant meeting places—"Just meet me at the Science Center," "I'll be in front of Annenberg"—or if you need a cheap lie, "I'm going all night at the Science Center."

I use the front entrance, not as instructed. William James Hall is more developed than the other buildings, and as a result, less detailed. Its ugly modernity does not say "Harvard."

I ride the elevator down to where the classrooms are. With a ding, it opens to a quiet student lounge with orange sofas where Nora, Ted, and Mike swig from Styrofoam cups. They are plugged in, each watching a live video feed from laptops. Mike's screen displays two women talking to each other. Ted's displays a man and woman doing the same. It looks like interrogation footage.

"You're late," Nora says casually. She's wearing a lab coat for some reason.

"I had class."

"One volunteer had to leave. You're down to one couple."

"What do you mean I'm *down* to one?"

She gestures for me to sit and presents me with head-phones and a laptop. It displays a live feed of a woman sitting at a table in a room.

"I get it," I start. "So just watch a couple ask a bunch of questions, and then see if they fall in love, right?"

"Well, yes, and then . . ." Nora clears her throat. "Then you have to follow them on their first date."

I stare at her.

"There have been many experiments like this." Her tone is firm, as if she rehearsed this response. "But they all end in the laboratory. None are followed through in person. None observe the couples, after the experiment, on a date like this. We'll be the first."

"Can I ask why?"

"Extra credit."

"I don't want extra credit."

"Charlie, this group project is thirty percent of the grade. We fail this, we're already in the C-plus region."

I sigh, put the headphones over my neck, and wipe my hands.

The room I observe in the live feed is about the size of a Star-bucks bathroom. A woman sits by herself with a cup of tea, waiting for something. She wears an oversized checkered knit sweater. She has almond-shaped eyes that look around, like a lost animal would. She appears to be in her midtwenties.

The legs of my chair are imbalanced, so I rock diagonally back and forth as I watch her like a certified pervert. She looks into the camera and waves. I wave. She can't see me, but she must know someone is behind that blinking red dot.

The door in her room clacks open and startles us both.

A man with Macklemore hair walks in with a distinctive strut. Subtle bumps of muscle protrude under his clothes.

"Hello." The woman sort of laughs at herself. I laugh with her.

"Hey, how's it going? I'm Wade."

"Nice to meet you, Wade. I'm Camilla." Her voice is sensitive and not loud.

"Camilla. Is that Russian?"

What an opener, Wade. They both sit with suppressed blushes, her more than him. He seems like the kind of guy who handles embarrassment with a kind of accidental cool.

Nora enters their room and gives them each an electronic wristband to track their heart rates.

"Your time starts now." Nora dampens her tone like a yoga instructor. "Read the questions on the clipboard and begin when you're ready. If you want to end the session at any time, just tell the camera. Any questions?"

None. Nora closes the door, winking at the camera on the way out.

Wade looks around for an excuse. "So, I guess we're on the clock now?"

"Yep. On the clock." Camilla glances down, holding in a laugh.

"So . . ." He looks at the clipboard, imitating her amusement. "Intimate details. You want to start?"

"Okay." She speaks with two dimples. "How about we introduce ourselves first?"

"Yes, please," I say to the screen.

"Cool," he shrugs.

"Hello, I'm Camilla." She waves. "I'm twenty-nine, and I'm originally from Oregon. I'm doing my master's in twentieth-century literature."

Wade does the "rock on" gesture. His necklace with a coin at the end of it clacks against the table.

"Dating never ends well for me, so now I'm here, wondering what I'm doing and what's wrong with me. Because I really don't know." Camilla rearranges the cup in front of her, slightly to the left, blushing.

Wade searches the ceiling, scratching his chin. "Nice, I love Oregon."

They ask their questions: What's the perfect day? What do you value in a friendship? Do you feel your childhood was

happier than other people's? I'm distracted by his answers, an-
swering the questions myself while Wade is talking. As insane
as it sounds, the questions have at least some effect. The more
I hear from Camilla, the more I want to know.

Absolutely no chemistry, I write in the notes. *Wade is without doubt a mere product of a weak pullout game.*

Thirty minutes later, a buzzer goes off, and they look at
the clock, then into the camera.

"I guess this is where we stare at each other?" Wade asks.

"For four minutes, I think." Camilla purses her lips.

"Four minutes. That's intense."

"Okay, let's do it."

He puts his hands on the table while she hides hers be-
neath it. They stare. No clocks, no phones, no traffic, only
naked silence and eye contact. I balance on the legs of my chair.

They stare without expression, completely still. Maybe
this is the secret to the whole experiment, this four-minute
stare. This is what no one else sees. Public life requires
wearing the attachable face of one's environment. But here,
the only face they wear is their own. Total acceptance of
the other.

What seems like only one minute later, a buzzer sounds.
Wade and Camilla look down with pinkish faces, saying nothing. Nora knocks and enters the room with a bright look.

"Camilla, Wade, how was that?"

Wade spills his guts. "She's amazing, wow. She's really great. Probably the greatest."

Nora interviews them about their physical states when they were asked certain questions, and then explains that they are now free to do whatever they want—go on a date, not go on a date, whatever. She thanks them for participating and shows them the exit, sticking her tongue out at the camera.

I take the headphones off.

"That was strange," I say to the air.

"Did any of yours ask each other out?" Ted asks behind his screen.

"Mine both did," says Mike, playing solitaire on his computer. "Lesbian couple and a straight couple."

I don't know whether I want this experiment to work or not. A familiar feeling of confusion and curiosity hits me, like when I know I will change by the end of a book I'm reading, but I don't know how just yet.

Nora emerges behind me, jolting me. She's thrilled: every test subject came out wanting a first date, including Wade and Camilla.

"Good," I mumble.

"This means you're on! I've told them you'll be observing them," Nora says, fiddling with some documents. "They've signed all the waivers."

"Good."

"Oh, and this goes for all of you," she addresses the room. "It's very important that you don't speak to either person while on their date."

"Why?" I ask, a little too excited.

"In order for the data to come out legitimate, they need to feel uninhibited by you," she explains. "The only way I convinced the board is if you, the volunteers, have zero verbal contact with the subjects. You must become flies on the wall."

"A fly on the wall," I mutter. "Invisible, anonymous, a third wheel, forgotten—what else would you like to know about my childhood?"

The first date is the next night. I wear a corduroy suit jacket and jeans like I'm in an '80s sitcom. I have this scenario in my head of Camilla realizing Wade's staleness and falling into my arms under the moonlight. How I'm going to accomplish this without words, I don't know. Nora isn't kidding about the no-talking part. If the subjects report that we "observers" talked during their date, the data will be deemed void, resulting in the instant failure of our group. Nora is carrying this whole crew; I can't go letting her down.

I wait under a starlit sky outside Felipe's, the restaurant where my couple is to enhance the chemical process of releasing dopamine and endorphins. An accordionist plays an obscure Dutch song. A grumpy pipe-smoking man sits in an office chair in front of the train station with an Allow Smoking petition sign. I don't see many signatures.

Clipboard in hand, I adjust my "observer" lanyard so it doesn't look so obvious.

I spot the royal couple. She wears a beige coat and scarf. He wears a leather jacket. His legs bulge in his calf-hugging pants. They look nervous—first-date jitters. As they step into the restaurant, I approach from behind and clear my throat.

Camilla turns to me. "Hi."

I show my lanyard, as if begging for money.

"Oh, you're the guy," she says.

"No way, this is the dude recording us?" Wade asks. "Rock on, man."

He offers a fist bump. I accidentally high-five it.

Felipe's is a well-known hangout for dates. Everyone has someone to laugh with, so I'm clearly out of place here: a single guy dressed like a 1983 CNN news anchor in the most unsingle place in Cambridge. This damned clipboard, I think that's the problem.

Wade and Camilla chat about their day. I stand behind them in line. He gets a burrito bowl, and she gets fish tacos. I get a bottle of Mexican Coke and put it on Wade's tab.

We sit at a table for three upstairs, and I quickly see that my presence makes things uncomfortable. Camilla and Wade are stilted for the first five minutes, commenting on

the interior of the restaurant. I make no movements. I just sit
there like a good boy and observe—a fly on the wall.

They make light of the situation.

"Would you like something else to drink?" Wade asks
her. "Tea, coffee . . . ?"

I grin at him and make an obvious show of taking notes.

"So, what'd you study in college?" Wade starts. The guy
is a real firecracker with the openers.

"I majored in literature and minored in music."

"Nice. That must be really interesting."

They go on a long run of "nice" and "oh wow." Camilla
asks more questions than Wade does. He offers a few nuggets
of an interesting past, and she explores them, though he tells
her nonchalantly, like he doesn't care who hears his secrets.

I'm guessing my facial expressions are obvious. I often
squint at the saltshaker after an inane comment by Wade. He
quit the piano after two years because it was "pretty annoy-
ing." But he found it "neat" that she plays.

"What's your favorite book?" Camilla asks.

She glances at me because I keep giving her the eye, but
she tries to ignore me.

"I mean I'm mostly into baseball stuff, but I liked this
one book called *The 4-Hour Workweek*. Do you know it?"

"Yeah, of course."

"It was pretty good. That, and *Rich Dad Poor Dad*."

"What's your music, what do you listen to?" she asks.

"Trap." Wade makes his favorite "rock on" gesture. "You?"

"Oldies. Jazz," she says. "This one jazz number I love—nuts, what's it called . . ."

I stop writing.

"Ugh, I hate when I forget it. It was in a Betty Boop cartoon . . ."

It's "Minnie the Moocher." Cab Calloway. I twist a napkin in self-restraint.

"I don't really know," Wade laughs. She laughs with him, to make things easy. My empty stare fills with a moody glaze. Wade pretends he doesn't notice.

Wade invites Camilla for "wine" back at his place. This shocks her. I lower my glasses at him, attempting the best parent face I can muster.

"I live in Seaport," he says. "I have a sick view of the ocean."

"Oh, Seaport." Camilla glances in my direction. I raise an eyebrow as if to say, *Can you believe this guy?* "I don't know. I have an early morning."

"Where do you live?"

"Here, about ten minutes away."

"Oh cool, let's go to your place then."

My neck juts forward. I can't believe the gall of this guy.

"I mean . . ." She fidgets with a napkin and then gestures to me. "He has to stay with us, you know. Those are the rules."

I throw my hands up as if to say *Sorry, the higher powers write the rules.*

"Let's bring him along. You down, man?" I shake my head.

Wade doesn't expect my answer, but he recovers quickly. "Oh. Well, okay. It's a free country, so I guess if you're not down, that's kind of on you."

"Don't do anything that makes you feel uncomfortable," Camilla tells me.

This is unbelievable.

"We'll get an Uber." Wade hands her his phone. "Punch in your address and let's get out of here."

I can't help but laugh at this strategy. Nice try, Wade, but you're going to have to do better than Spartan biceps and enough confidence to light up a cave. He clearly doesn't understand the female psyche.

In the Uber I anxiously reserve the middle seat, forcing a barrier between the two. Wade asks if I can scoot a little so he can put on his seatbelt. I shrug. I don't know, Wade, can I?

The driver plays Elton John's "Tiny Dancer," and Wade attempts to make this a moment. He grabs for Camilla's hand, crossing over my lap, and lip-syncs the song with an imaginary microphone. She laughs and plays along. Damn it, she

laughed. It's over. What does she see in this bozo, unbeliev-
ably good looks?

She'll probably call it a night the second she gets out of
the car.

In the elevator, Camilla fidgets with her keys. The cogs squeak,
and the buttons are faded. The doors open to a barren hallway
with a few welcome mats and the smell of curry fumigating.
Our steps are awkwardly quiet.

Camilla lives in a studio across from the Business School,
overlooking the Charles River. I know this apartment complex. Grad students live here.

"Would you like some coffee?" she offers both of us.

Her place smells like jasmine.

"Yeah, cool." Wade takes off his jacket.

I offer Camilla an apologetic look. She grins back, recognizing the humor of the situation. My urge to speak, regulated
by guilt. I want to tell her so much, to tell her this guy isn't
worth it. But Wade will surely be sore at me for that, and
he'll no doubt snitch and derail the whole study.

Wade and I take seats on the sofa. We don't look at each
other. Camilla's room is lined with café lights. I can't believe
what I see on her bookshelf: *Catch-22*, *West with the Night*,
Testament of Youth, *Breakfast at Tiffany's*. It's like our taste
buds were copied and pasted from the same DNA. She owns

a record player. Some vinyl records lay around: Ray Conniff
Singers, Louis Armstrong, Nina Simone—this is killing me.

Without asking, Wade turns on the news. A former bank
robber in Malden wrote a children's book and now wants to
run for city council.

"Here you go." She gives us our coffee and in a final
blow, the mugs she serves are decorated with famous lines in
cinema. She sits between us on the sofa. We sip our coffee,
watching the news.

"I had a really good time tonight," Wade says.

She turns to him. "Likewise."

He gives her a hug. I clear my throat. He strategically
opens one button of his shirt. In his white shirt, without a
sweater, I see the full perfection of his pectoral muscles.

"I think we're really good together, you know?" Wade
puts his arm around her shoulder. His tactlessness comes off
as genuine, but if he were uglier, it'd be awkward.

"I mean, yeah, I like where this is going." Camilla offers
a nervous giggle.

"I feel like I can talk to you for hours."

"Yeah," she agrees reluctantly. I make note of how pun-
gent his cologne is.

"Have you ever been in love?" she asks him.

"Yeah, I think so. But, you know, my last girlfriend really
hurt me."

"Oh yeah?"

"Yeah." He puts on a sympathetic tone. "She was crazy. She cheated on me with the janitor at her office."

Very original, Wade.

"Oh my God, Wade. Really?"

"Yeah. She just ripped my heart right out of my chest. Then she threw it on the ground, stomped on it with her high heels, and played soccer with it before lighting it on fire and throwing it in the recycling bin."

Yes, thank you for that, Wade.

"Jesus . . ."

"I never thought I could feel again . . ." He hugs her, and she hugs back, moaning a motherly hum.

I write in my notes: *What the hell, Wade?*

This last hug doesn't end. His arms find their way down her waist. Her hands crawl up to his hair. I clear my throat again. She kisses his neck.

I try to keep my eyes on the TV. The Roxbury School District is petitioning the city of Boston to change the Slow Children at Play sign, as it is offensive to the disabled and, frankly, bad grammar. Wade groans, and his shirt takes a vacation from his body. In other news, it sounds like broccoli is still good for you. After much speculation over its health benefits, the FDA has unofficially classified it as a superfood. However, top nutritionists are still looking into whether steaming or boiling affects the nutrients. Camilla's hair whips me in the face. Another UFO has been spotted in Florida, during the day, this time hovering over a nude beach in Miami. Officials are not releasing footage of the unidentified object until further investigation is completed and all genitalia can be blurred. Camilla and Wade gasp for air. A new species of tree kangaroo has been discovered in the Philippines today. Wade tugs her hair. Biologists claim the new species might reveal how the animal evolved in the region and its relationship to prehistoric dinosaurs. They're rolling around on the sofa. Some paleontologists disagree with these findings, pending further evidence.

I stand up and carry my coffee mug to the sink. I open Camilla's door and leave. Before I shut it, I hear, "Oh, he's leaving," but I don't know who whispers it. The hallway is a dense kind of quiet. I can almost hear my pulse. I lean against a wall, staring at my reflection in a framed picture of fruit.

A familiar feeling arrives. I knew it was coming. The idea spreads through me—the idea that perhaps I am someone I don't like. I've become the nice-guy trope. Duckie from *Pretty in Pink*. A Ross Geller, a Ted Mosby. I've become that guy who tries to nice his way into a girl's bedroom. I hate this guy as much as anyone, and I'm him. Delicate, moral-posturing, Wade-hating, resentful him.

I've become a cliché.

I want to die, but I'm so unlucky that if I were reincarnated, I'd probably just come back as myself.

On Friday I go to Lamont to give my report to Nora.

In the café, she mingles over Mike's and Ted's reports over a café au lait that does not emit steam. When she sees me, she gives me a hug to relieve her stress, which I flinch at, distressed by the idea of hugs since the other night. Nora apologizes, and I tell her not to worry, it's no big deal. She says no, that I shouldn't repress my feelings. I say you're right, back off.

"What's this?" I pick out an index card with a list of questions.

"Oh, the 'falling in love' questions." Nora takes a sip of her cold coffee.

"Huh. So, Nora, how have you grown emotionally this year?" I read from the card.

"You can have it if you want."

"I'll try it on my History of Agnosticism TA." I slip the card into a pocket. "So that's it. It's over. We're done, right?"

"We're done." Nora closes her eyes. All anxiety seems to have left her face.

"What's this experiment supposed to prove, anyway? I mean, who cares if people fall in love that quick?"

"I don't know. It demystifies love, maybe." She rubs her

temples. "If anyone can love anyone, what's so special about love? Perhaps in the end, it's just dopamine, oxytocin, and red wine, all occurring at the right time with the right questions. Something like that."

I take a nibble from her muffin.

"Have you ever been in love?" I ask after a pause. This takes her aback.

"Yes."

She doesn't clarify, so I don't push. My thoughts float away. We talk about topics that don't matter, like whether broccoli should be boiled or steamed. She tells me how her family is doing and where she wants to travel for winter break.

"How are the shoes?" she asks. I got new shoes before the semester started.

"They still hurt."

"They hurt me just looking at them."

We got a failing grade on the assignment. The reasoning went on for three pages in eleven-point font, formally scorning each of us: myself, Mike, Ted, and Nora, individually and collectively. There was apparently an obvious ethical breach in our research method, a lack of written permission from the professor, plagiarism—there have been numerous "falling in love studies," and our love questions strikingly resembled a 2015 *New York Times* article called "The 36 Questions That Lead to Love"—and on top of all this, Ted spoke on one of the dates.

I reconsider whether psychology is really for me.

On a Thursday, at 11:39 p.m., I drift down Mt. Auburn Street after seeing a showing of *E.T.* at Brattle Theater. I come across a group of pigeons congregating near the late-night chess players in front of the train station. I stand in the middle of their assembly as a lonely violinist plays inside the station. His song echoes as if in a cave. The pigeons peck around my stiff shoes in their never-ending search for crumbs. Perhaps they think they will someday find one outstanding breadcrumb that lasts them their entire lives and they would never again search for the pettiness of common crumbs. They would find their one crumb and keep it forever.

As my eyes come back into focus, I see the Girl Named Camilla walking into CVS, alone. I take a deep breath and follow. Her earth-tone sweater flutters up the stairs.

She lands in the oral-hygiene section, where I approach her slowly, my shoes squeaking. My forbidden moment: we are finally alone. I stand there, pretending to browse for a new tongue scraper.

"Oh." She recognizes me. "Hi."

"Oh, hey!" I act surprised.

She looks around. "Wow, we haven't really met, but I guess the experiment is over, so we can talk now?"

"Sure, absolutely." My fingers nervously writhe into each other. "How are you?"

"I'm good, just working on my thesis, you know how that goes." Her shoulder cranks up as if whatever trial she is going through is and was always unimportant.

"Are you and Wade . . . ?"

"Oh no, that was just a thing." With a flick of her hand, Wade never existed.

"By the way, 'Minnie the Moocher,'" I say. She looks confused. "The song you were trying to remember, the one in the Betty Boop cartoon."

"Oh, of course!" We walk to the hair products together. "You remember that?"

"Are you kidding, I had so much to say to you."

"Really? Like what?"

"Just that . . . you know . . ." I'm blanking. "You have great taste in music."

"Oh, thank you—"

"And books, you have great taste in books as well."

"You were so quiet I didn't know you were paying attention." She checks the back of a bottle of conditioner. "So are you . . ." She searches for the words. "Are you a grad student?"

"Me? No, no. Undergrad."

"Right," she says. "What are you studying?"

"Psychology, in theory." I wring my hands and pick out some makeup removers. I thought the magic would be better than this. What happened to all those great things I had to say to her?

I put a hand in my pocket, and my fingernails wedge into a bent-up, folded index card. The "love questions." I realize I can ask her one.

We stand in the checkout line, chatting about the other night, exchanging obvious observations about Wade.

"You know, it's funny," she tells me. "When Wade was babbling on about . . . God knows what, I just kept thinking to myself: What does falling in love look like? I forgot. You get to a point where you can't tell anymore if you're throwing away an opportunity."

I hold still and listen.

"But then, maybe I never knew what falling in love looked like. Maybe that's why I've always picked the wrong guy, because I always thought it was my loss if I left."

The line moves forward.

"I guess it looks different for everyone," I say. "For some it's *wham!* First sight. And others, it starts as friends."

"I certainly know what it doesn't look like," she says. "It wasn't then, with him."

And neither is it now, with her. I wish it looked like now,

but I know it doesn't. When I was ten, my parents sent me to Dr. Groban for my yearly checkup. At the end of the appointment, he asked if I had any questions. I asked him what an orgasm feels like. I'd been trying to get one for weeks. Uncomfortable as hell, he lowered his glasses and said, "You'll know when you know."

And I guess the same goes for caring and being cared about. Everyone wants it; it's the only thing that makes life tolerable. We keep trying to get it, but in the end, "You'll know when you know."

On a Tuesday at 10:51 p.m., I contemplate the could've beens over pancakes. Today has just been one of those days. Gray, foggy, imagining what might have happened if only I'd made braver choices. I could have easily run away with the circus. I'd have started off as a tightrope walker and worked my way up to being one of those clowns with trust issues, and after some serious networking, been promoted to a magician who could make anything vanish except his regrets: if only he had asked her out at the senior dance, if only he had caught that ball in the final seconds of the game—maybe life would've been different.

I sit with Nora, Mike, and Ted at a place called Zoe's Diner in Central Square, where the smell of cigarettes and pancakes—the smell of America—wafts through the late-night air. Some foreign soccer game plays in the kitchen, where the Colombian line cooks occasionally cheer. The faint sound of jazz floats from the speaker system: Teddy Wilson's "Our Love Is Here to Stay." We linger in our failing grade, our bad beginning to our sophomore year. Nora says she'd rather fail with friends than win with strangers, but Mike says it'd be better just to win with friends, to which no one has a response.

After we gorge on our pancakes and coffee, no one says anything for a while. Failure feels like it lasts forever on Tuesdays. I thought I'd be good at so many things when I was younger, only to grow up and find out how hard it is to be good at even one thing. It's just been one of those days.

"Do you believe in soulmates?" Nora suddenly asks us, breaking the trance.

"I used to, then I didn't, and now I do again," says Mike, crumbling up a straw wrapper.

"I don't believe in 'em," I say. "It isn't even a romantic idea. I mean, if you meet your soulmate, you'd be crazy not to wind up with them, wouldn't you?

"But you know that somewhere, there's someone that seamlessly matches your combination of traits," says Nora.

"So what?"

"So, call it soulmates or don't, someone is out there who is scientifically perfect for you." She dips a strawberry into a small bowl of whipped cream but doesn't eat it. "Your desires harmonize. Your insecurities are such that you can't judge each other for them. And they're out there somewhere, just like you, wondering where you are."

"What's really special to me is choice," I say. "If it's all left to chance, that means you, out of seven billion dots in the world, chose this dot. It's the conscious, dumb choice that makes it beautiful."

Mike audibly slurps his cold decaf from a green mug. His expression is stoic. "Why do you think this generation is so unsatisfied?" He avoids eye contact with anyone. "Why'd our parents never have a phase of quitting their jobs to start a side hustle in cookie dough?"

Ted chimes in with his theory. "It was probably something in our tap water."

"Or maybe the promise that you could have it all," Nora says, drawing something on her plate with the cream-tipped strawberry. "That you could be anything you wanted if you believed hard enough."

"Yeah, where'd that come from?" Ted asks. "I can't even manifest groceries, much less life goals. Even the slightest possibility that things could be better drives me nuts."

"I don't know what I miss anymore," I say, not looking anyone in the eye. "I miss something, though. Why does it always feel like I'm missing something? I'll spend an hour deciding on something to watch. By the time I choose

something, I'm asleep. I feel like it's some big metaphor for
my life. Just last week I asked for a ten percent discount at
that café, Peets, because I go there so much. They gave it to
me. Now I'm kicking myself. If I got that, I could've gotten
more. You know, at this point, 'better' isn't good enough.
'Good enough' isn't enough. 'Enough' is not enough."

There comes a certain hour and mood, in empty diners
with coffee, when confessions can be safely transmitted to
nonjudgmental ears. It's gotten pretty late and, without formally acknowledging it, we decide it is time to return to
campus. The walk back to Harvard Square is a good twenty
minutes, but we do it, drunk on thoughts of life and love.
As we walk down Mass Avenue whistling Les Brown's "Senti-
mental Journey," an unfamiliar feeling of permanence blooms
up in me, as if I'm aware of a core memory being crystalized
into my brain.

So, on these days, I do what I gotta do—confide in a stray
cat, eat pancakes for dinner, and watch a comedy, all until
I am reminded that this isn't forever. My only regret is that
I regretted everything up until now. Life could have turned
out any number of ways, but it's a game of Whac-A-Mole:
every way it could have turned out comes with problems.
Nora once told me the important thing is a sense of humor.
That if you don't have a sense of humor in this world, you'll
die. That if you can't laugh, it'll always be Tuesday. Everyone

wants to feel justified for their inconveniences. That's all anybody wants. That, and free parking.

"Night," Mike yells, not turning back as he heads to his dorm.

"*Bonne nuit*, all." Nora waves off.

Ted doesn't say anything to anyone and just disappears down Plympton Street.

We've got to make the most of the memories we have. Small blips we grow up brushing off as mundane moments or "not really love" are all we have, aren't they? So that's reality for you, as normal and tame as it seems. It's all we got. Most of our lives would fill a small novel. A small, stupid, beautiful little novel.

getting there

(october)

It is Friday and already October, and I can hear voices outside the window, people going places. Everyone is going someplace. Being young and unafraid is about just that, multiple acts of pointless wandering concluded by some life lesson you already learned at twelve. My dental hygienist once said that life is a continuous chapter of accidents, but sometimes there are good accidents called "Wow, what great weather." I'm inclined to agree with that midwestern simplicity.

"*Charlie!*"

Oh my God, the kid must have cut his finger off. I bolt to the stairs, my socks skidding, and step on a Lego halfway down. My shin dings a railing. I run to the kitchen. The refrigerator is open.

"What's wrong?" My lungs burn.

A seven-year-old boy sits on a plush sofa, bouncing up

and down the way children do. The flicker of a televangelist on TV changes the tint of his small, giggly face.

"What is it?" I ask again.

"I'm bored."

A fly buzzes around the open jar of Nutella on his lap and then lands, leaving only the sound of the televangelist clarifying why Jesus would have flown business class, too. I limp over and change the channel to some violent cartoon.

"Again, whenever you're bored, you can just change the channel," I explain, as calmly as possible.

"Okay."

"You press this button right here—Johm, are you paying attention? This button." I point to it.

"Okay." He balances a fidget spinner on his thumb.

"If we're bored, what do we do?"

No answer.

"We change the . . ."

He picks his nose. "Temperature?"

"The channel, we change the channel, Johm."

"Okay."

My decision to babysit for the day is a direct result of American income inequality. I'm doing someone a small favor, but it's neither small nor just anyone. Dennis Haswell is the head of Financial Services at Harvard, and he's the kind of man who rolls belts into coils and wraps rubber bands around

them. He knows me very well, but not by choice. I haggled
with Dennis during my first semester about help with tuition. This semester was an inconvertible "no."

Then, two weeks into the semester, while I was giving
myself a foot massage, I got a call.

"Charlie, how are you?"

"I'm okay, Dennis. How's Tahiti?"

He ignored this. "I spoke to the board, and though they
weren't exactly thrilled to handle this during their vaca-
tions"—he cleared his throat—"it looks like we'll be able to
pay at least half your tuition this semester."

"You're kidding, really?"

"It's not set in stone, but the odds are in your favor."

"I can't thank you enough. I really owe you one,
Dennis. I—"

"Actually," he interjects. He was ready for this. "I need
you to housesit and watch my son for a few days."

"Oh," I blinked. Who the hell takes people up on the
I-owe-you-one thing? "Like, babysitting?"

"My wife and I won't be back until the twenty-first, and
the sitter has a wedding on the twentieth."

"You can't find another sitter?" I accidentally asked. A
pause went by.

"Why, is it a problem?" It sounded like a threat. My
financial aid wasn't "set in stone," after all. Harvard's

thirty-nine-billion-dollar endowment fund allows Dennis
to give the financial aid I need like mints on Halloween. I see
his logic. Through me, he won't need to pay for a new, expensive sitter; Harvard will. Very under the books, I assume.

Dennis's townhouse is on Newberry Street. While a
measly studio apartment in Cambridge costs $2,500 a month,
this place goes three floors up. A rich home to myself, overlooking the Boston Commons, for a whole day . . . It would
be a terrific deal if it weren't for Johm. Dennis couldn't have
named his son John, for that would be too common. The
linguistic complexity of Johm is intended to suggest sophis-
tication, I think, but Johm is hardly sophisticated. The kid
complains of hospital-level emergencies and his imminent
boredom in the same tone.

I prepare myself in the guest room, putting on a vinyl copy
of Bob Dylan's *Blood on the Tracks* album from Dennis's col-
lection. I stare into the mirror, practicing my "interested"
expression for my date. Like most hours before dates, I get
nervous and think about who I am and what I've become
and where I put the mouthwash.

Shortly after I was bribed into housesitting yesterday,
I managed to arrange myself a date. Dates are partly life
assessments, but as Seinfeld says, they're mostly job interviews—and you either get the job or you don't.

But this is no ordinary job interview; it's with Miranda Maxwell, an old-money Manhattanite. On paper, she's the absolute Harvard type. She studies biology, almost made the Olympic pole-vaulting team, performs competitively as a concert oboist, and in her senior year started a charity for retired sumo wrestlers. And she is beautiful, yes. I know well that Miranda Maxwell has been involved with Harvard's top athletes and inevitable Wall Street billionaires. So why she agreed to a date with me is beyond comprehension. Was she bored, or desperate? With my romantic luck, I can't afford to ask.

When I asked Miranda to dinner and she said "yes," it was the worst good news I could receive. Now comes the question of who will watch Johm.

As I knot up a navy-blue knit tie, the doorbell rings. I hobble downstairs, shirt untucked, and open the front door.

"I had a bad dream, and now I'm having a crisis." A panicked Nora steps into the house like she rehearsed it. This is not the ideal opening line from a friend you call to cover your back while you go chase romance.

"Now?"

"What am I doing with myself? What am I going to do with my degree?" Nora paces. "Do you realize all we're doing as a human species is solving problems? We're problem-solving for no reason. Why do the problems even exist?"

"You couldn't figure this out before you got here?" I try to unjam my fly.

"Hitler—if God exists, why did he allow Hitler?"

"How the hell do I know why he allowed Hitler? I can't zip my fly."

"Gelato." Nora tangles her hands and marches to the kitchen. "I need gelato."

"Hey, are you okay to watch the kid while I'm gone?" I follow her.

"Kids, that's another thing . . . Do I want kids? We don't know why we're here, what this is all for, but we keep creating new human beings to live in it. Oh, this dream was terrible, I need to tell you about it."

"Nora, I appreciate your attempt to figure out all of humanity here, but this is probably not the optimal attitude for a babysitter."

She pulls out a pint of Cherry Garcia and shovels it with a tablespoon.

"Maybe I should go back to church." Her lean, giraffe-like body can never be still when nervous. "I haven't been to confessional in years. What would I confess now? I'd probably tell him everything that has ever happened to me, just to be safe."

"Fascinating, I'll go with you to cosign." I gesture her to the living room. "This is Johm. Hey, Johm, this is Nora, she's going to watch you for a bit while I'm gone, okay?"

Johm is unfazed. Nora must seem like any other nanny in his rich little life. I take her to the sofa, ice cream still in her hands, and suggest she watch *SpongeBob* with Johm.

"Hello, Johm." Nora's body is stiff.

"Hi," he says, with a spoon in his mouth. I think he might be taken by the fact she correctly pronounced his name on the first try. He gazes at her without inhibition, and this makes Nora's cheeks twitch, faintly and briefly.

"I've been noticing all the ways I'm coping with reality," she continues, staring at Johm like he's a museum exhibit. "I want to start all over as a baby. Forget everything so far ever happened."

My date is in one hour and my babysitter-double is questioning her place in the universe. "Well, you can start with Cartoon Network."

"Adulthood is punishment for all the fun you had in childhood," she says.

I sneak off upstairs, leaving her rambling.

I dress in a tweed blazer with black pants, and I smell great, hopefully. I booked a reservation at Casablanca, a dining experience well beyond my wallet, but for Miranda Maxwell, it's probably just dinner, so compromises have been made.

"I'm going to take a bath," Nora says at my room door. "Everything looks better after a bath."

"Good idea. And you know, watching him isn't much," I point downstairs, referring to Johm. "He just wants to watch TV and eat Nutella."

She stares off into the distance. "Don't we all?"

I put down the cologne. "Hey, are you okay? I'm sorry I didn't ask earlier. You look pale."

"Maybe after the bath I'll be okay. Can I tell you about my dream?"

"I have to go."

"Oh." Her eyes glaze across the floor.

"How do I look?"

"Yeah. Good."

Good means not repulsive. I can work with not repulsive. She slumps off into one of the two bathrooms as I dab on some concealer for men. I can hear the bath running, and Nora starts crooning out some French song.

I stare at my face in the mirror, an existential experience if you stare long enough, and for a brief window of about a second or two, I like myself. Everything is right. Life is looking up.

Then the fire alarm goes off.

As with most fire alarms, I give it a second. It might be a mistake. Nora stops singing. Five seconds. Ten seconds. The sound doesn't vanish the way postmodern problems should.

"Charlie?" Nora yells from the bath.

"I'll check, probably a false alarm." I finger my heel into some leather shoes. "The fire department is on their way."

"They're what?"

"Dennis said if any alarm goes off, they come automatically. They're rich, Nora."

I hear her curse in French, and then the squeaking sound of skin against porcelain. I do a wallet-and-keys check. Nora steps out in a bathrobe, her hair in a towel.

I run down to retrieve Johm. He's covered his ears with two pillows while trying to watch a Mattress Firm infomercial. The stove is off, the oven is off, nothing in the microwave, no candles lit—the house seems clean. I don't smell smoke.

Nora sprinkles foot powder into her shoes. I remind her that inferno is a far more pertinent threat than foot fungus.

"This better be real," she threatens, a very odd wish.

For all her nihilistic angst, Nora assumes her sitter duties like a real Mary Poppins, making sure Johm's little jacket is zipped to the chin. She takes his hand and brings him outside. He's brought his teddy bear, but he wants her to hold it.

The fire department arrives with medium- to low-range urgency.

A mustached firefighter with a slit of a frown between his caterpillar eyebrows approaches. "All right, folks, we're just going to do a routine check and let you know if it's safe to go inside."

"I didn't see anything," I inform him. He ignores this.

"I'm hungry," Johm announces.

Nora shivers at the autumn wind, clutching the front of her robe. "What would you like?"

"I don't know."

"I can make toast."

"I had toast for breakfast."

"I can make breakfast."

"For dinner?" Johm picks his nose and rubs it on her robe.

"Why not? Pancakes, crepes?" She rubs his hair. "Why must they start the day but not end it?"

Johm leans against her leg.

I keep an eye on the time. My ride should be arriving in five minutes. My driver is named Felix.

The fire alarm goes quiet, and I turn to the fire chief, hopeful. His expression doesn't change. A single firefighter comes jogging out the front door and whispers something to the fire chief. The fire chief whispers something back.

I interject their bro moment for the sake of time. "Is everything . . . ?"

He turns to the three of us like he's addressing a town hall. "Well, the good news is we've identified the problem. The bad news is, it's not a fire."

This is the strangest thing I've ever heard from a fireman.

"So, false alarm?" I ask.

"Nope. That was the carbon monoxide detector."

"Isn't that the thing that kills you?" I ask.

"Lots of things can kill you, son." He looks me in the eye as he delivers these lines. "I would suggest you and your family check into a hotel."

"Hang on, how long is this going to take?"

"At least an hour, two hours, maybe."

A breeze whistles by in the silence.

"Where are we going to go?" Nora asks.

"I'm hungry." Johm is still picking his nose.

The fire chief takes my number, promising to call when it's safe to return. I receive a notification that Felix, my driver, is around the corner. Nora and Johm look like a mother-son wartime refugee duo.

"You know," I turn to them. "Pancakes sound like a great idea. Why don't we go to IHOP?"

"Oh, IHOP." Nora tilts her head, fascinated by this suggestion. "You're joking, right? Very funny? Ha, ha, ha? I'm in a robe, Charlie."

"Where else is there, the YMCA? I can't think of anywhere that'll be open in two hours except there and McDonald's."

Nora suggests the dorms, but all Veritas-encrusted buildings are a no-go. Any Harvard faculty member, even an old security guard, recognizing Johm from Dennis's "take your kid to work" day is bound to lead to questions. As we race-walk

around the corner to where Felix is parked, I try to convince
Nora that she's dressed fine for IHOP. She argues in short,
feisty steps, gripping Johm's hand. He looks like Paddington
Bear stuffed into that coat. I find the car, a 1990s minivan,
and we cram into the back, Johm in the middle.

"What kind of a man are you, abandoning your child and
co-babysitter at the International House of Pancakes?" Nora
grumbles, securing Johm's seatbelt, and then his teddy bear's.

The car smells like a dollar store. I tell Felix to drop us
off at IHOP, four or five blocks from Casablanca. He is the
silent type and doesn't even confirm the name. We're at A,
and whoever hops in, he's taking them to B, no questions
asked. He turns on his screamo metal and drives. Nora mutters French profanities under her breath.

"Have a good night," I wish Felix. He offers one brief wave.

We step into the crisp October air, once again reminded
that reality has a windchill. In fifteen minutes I am to meet
Miranda Maxwell. It is a six-minute walk to Casablanca from
here.

The IHOP near the Kennedy School of Government is
open until 3:00 a.m., when no other affordable establishment
is. Two-thirds of the tables are occupied with a zoo of diners.
Three cops sit in one booth, and next to them is a table of
Harvard seniors in suits, returning from a party. Construction

workers doing the late shift, in for a lunch break of chicken and waffles. A clatter of noise from both throaty Boston accents and accentless college types.

"Can I help you?" the manager asks us.

This is neither the greeting nor the tone of a man welcoming us into his business but of one wondering why a James Bond wannabe, a woman in a robe, and a kid walked into his restaurant.

"Table for three," I request.

He looks down at Nora's attire, his stern tiger eyes pondering my request like it's a negotiation. After an uncomfortable three seconds, he snatches menus from under his lectern and walks to a corner booth without a word. We wriggle in. Decaf is brought to our table. I restrain, looking at my watch. Ten minutes till showtime.

Johm looks around. I doubt he's ever traveled this low in the social echelon. "Blue is my favorite color. Can we watch *Spider-Man* when we get back?"

"You're okay here for the next two hours?" I ask Nora, checking the time again.

"Where are you going?" Johm asks.

Nora chimes in. "He's going to see another woman."

"You're leaving us?"

"What—no, I'll be right back. Hey, don't tell him that." I look at Nora. Her eyes are glued to the menu.

"Don't you like us?" Johm asks. Jesus, this is getting out of hand.

"I'll be right back, I promise. And look, the second I get a call from the fire department, I'll order you both a car home, and then you can watch *Spider-Man*."

"What's your favorite color?"

"Green."

A waiter brings tap water to our table.

"I have to go. I'll be late even if I leave now."

"Ah yes, go. Go on your date, have a beautiful time with a beautiful girl while we wait here dropping carbohydrates into our bodies, pondering death," Nora rambles, pouring and stirring cream into her coffee.

As she reaches for another sugar packet, her left breast pops out of her robe. The waiter halts, holding his notebook halfway open about to take our order. It hangs there like Lady Liberty's in Eugène Delacroix's painting, *Liberty Leading the People*.

"But no, not for Charlie. Responsibility is not his friend. You take what you want when you want it—"

"Nora," I say.

"His desires are king. His vanity is poetry." She rips open more sugar and stirs.

"Nora," I say.

She looks up. I point at my chest, for reference. She looks

down. Like a snake striking for a mouse, she covers up and locks her wrist there in eye-bulging disbelief.

The waiter clicks his pen, puts his notebook into his apron, and walks to the front with no bounce in his step, like he's gliding. Nora clutches the front of her robe, holding her temple with the other hand.

"What are they doing?" She can't bear to look.

I turn around. The waiter returns with the manager, their faces tolerant but stern.

"Please leave the premises," the manager demands.

"Look, this was an honest mistake," I plead.

He steps aside and palm points to the exit. "Before I report this to the police. Please."

"It was nothing," Nora says. "No one saw anything."

"Please." He closes his eyes, gesturing to the exit.

"No one saw anything," I repeat. "It was out for what, three seconds? A boob is a boob."

"Boob or no boob, I want you all out! Out!" he yells. His baritone silences the room. All eyes twitch in our direction.

Knowing she cannot win this, Nora inhales through her nose and stands up.

"Let's go, Johm," she projects, loud enough for the whole room to hear. "It seems this establishment has a problem with the beauty of breastfeeding."

This earns a few mild gasps from the female diners, then

a hushed murmuring begins. The skin behind the manager's ears tightens. Holding Johm's fingers with one hand and the teddy bear with the other, Nora throws her shoulders back with pride and marches out. It would make for terrific TV if Oprah were here.

We're back outside. My reservation at Casablanca started three minutes ago. This is just beautiful, absolutely perfect.

"What was that?!" Nora cries. "What in the Jesus Christ was that? What kind of a man yells 'boob' in crowded place? That is not free speech, that's just terrible manners!"

Miranda Maxwell won't give me another chance, no matter what excuse I give. No woman buys an excuse from a man. It's just bad business. This will be another chapter in the series of disappointments that is my life. I am stuck in a loop of losses.

No, not again. I'm not giving in.

"I know where we can go," I tell Nora.

"Has the fire department called?"

"No, but in the meantime, I know somewhere we can wait."

Casablanca is one of those alleyway basement restaurants that tenured Harvard professors and wealthy students dine at. Waiters will give the "who are you" look. The place only just achieves the minimum legal lighting standards of a commercial establishment, which is great for getting drowsy with wine and passion, but terrible for dipping a french fry.

"Oh, by the way," Nora mentions as I speedwalk down the alley. "I'm sorry about your date."

"My what?"

"Your date. You were all dressed up."

"Oh, she'll understand." I look down in shame as I open the door for Nora and Johm.

Nora enters, but her momentum quickly slows. I rush the hostess before she can stare me down.

"Hi, I have a reservation for eight thirty under Charlie."

"Your table is ready, sir." The Russian hostess looks me judgmentally in the eye. "A member of your party is already seated."

Nuts, I look like an inept little boy who can't arrive on time. I'm praying Miranda doesn't see this as indicative of other aspects of myself.

"Charlie, what is this?" Nora asks.

"Also . . ." I nervously avoid her eyes and focus on the hostess. "We'll be adding two more diners tonight. Can we have two extra chairs?"

The hostess gives Nora the up-and-down. I can guess what she's thinking: this is either a homeless person or a celebrity. What will it be? After a four-second stare-off, the hostess unclenches her jaw and retrieves three menus. Celebrity it is.

"Right this way, please." She walks with the posture of a ballerina.

By all counts, this is probably the worst thing I've ever done to anyone, surpassing the whoopee cushion I left under the piano seat of my high school's valedictorian during a musical recital. My back is drenched with nervous sweat. As I am realizing what a mistake this is, I half consider ditching the whole evening. But then I see her, Miranda Maxwell, sitting alone at a candlelit table in the middle of the restaurant, her hair smoothly blond atop a classic black dress.

The world slows down. This is it.

"Hi, Miranda," I greet her, my arms diplomatically low, nice and cool.

"Hello." Her eyes land on Nora, and then Johm. "Oh, what's . . . ?"

"Oh! Forgive me. This is Nora and Johm—like John but with an *m*. Johm, Nora, this is Miranda Maxwell."

Nora swallows and sticks out her hand. Miranda stares at it and then shakes it. All is awkward.

A waiter brings the extra chairs in a studied dance. Johm is seated next to Miranda. His face just barely reaches the table.

"What about Fred?" he asks, pointing to his teddy bear.

"Can Fred stay on your lap tonight?" Nora quietly negotiates.

"I need a seat for Fred," Johm addresses the waiter directly, "one of those high ones so he can see the table." His brief, wealthy upbringing has trained him to ask for whatever he wants.

"Of course. One moment, please." The waiter disappears.

"Sorry for the wait, we had a carbon monoxide issue," I explain to Miranda.

"Carbon monoxide," she repeats, her neck stiff, almond eyes unblinking.

Nora breathes through her nose, also not blinking.

"Well, I see you've already ordered drinks," I say, trying to distract. "What are we drinking? Water?"

"Yes." Miranda Maxwell's eyes dart back and forth from me to Nora to Johm, trying to figure out what's going on.

The waiter returns with Fred's high chair, and either in jest or to make a good impression, he places a napkin on the doll's lap. A few diners look our way, amused.

"I'm a big water drinker," I say. "Do you like water?"

"Yes. Yes, I drink lots of water," Miranda says.

"That's good. Water is very good for you."

"I don't like water," Johm interjects. "I like grape juice." He plays with a spoon, putting it over the candle flame.

I calmly take the spoon and place it in front of him. "I drink water first thing in the morning. What about you, Miranda?"

Miranda places an elbow on the table. "I'm sorry, I don't mean to— Are these your friends?"

Johm picks up the spoon and places it over the flame.

"Well, I'm just babysitting Johm, you see." I take the spoon and place it back in front of him.

Miranda points her chin at Nora. "So, she's not your best friend or anything?"

I try to sound casual. "No, my best friend lives in Cleveland. He's a great guy, you'd love him."

We sit through a pained silence. Johm places his spoon over the flame.

"Would you like something to drink, sir?" the waiter asks.

"Yes!" I yell. Diners from other tables glance over. "I'll have what she's having."

"So, water?"

"Yes. Water. Are you drinking a special kind of water? Tap, distilled, spring?"

"Just water," she says.

"Just water then."

"I'll have chocolate milk," Johm demands.

"And you, ma'am?" The waiter makes no spectacle of Nora's attire.

Nora clears her throat. "I'll have a bottle of Merlot with an order of caviar and brie."

I deserve that.

The waiter marches off, his presence instantly missed. We linger in another painful bout of silence. The bossa nova music playing from the speakers somehow makes everything worse.

"So, how's it going?" I ask Miranda.

Her jaw is clenched. My hands are clamped together under the table, rekindling my religion, praying she doesn't ask why Nora is here and what the bathrobe is all about.

"I want dino nuggets," Johm says.

"We'll get you dino nuggets," Nora says, taking his spoon from the flame and placing it in front of him.

"You know that part in *Avengers* when Hulk turns big?" Johm says, bouncing restlessly in his seat. "How does Hulk's underwear stay on if the rest of his clothes rip off?"

My phone rings. I answer. It's the fire department. We're good to return home.

"That was the fire department," I announce. "They said the carbon monoxide problem is all taken care of."

Everyone blinks.

Knowing I can't delay the inevitable much longer, I decide to address everything. It's either that or I break down in tears.

"Let me just address the elephant in the room," I start.

"Thank you," Miranda says.

I take a deep breath, bracing myself.

"I want to tell you the truth, because I don't think this

night is going to last much longer without it. The truth is, I couldn't believe you would even give me a chance. You're smart, accomplished, and beautiful. I mean, look at me. I'm a liberal arts student who can't change a light bulb. I know a date is so simple to you, but for a guy like me, you never forget things like this. This is the stuff that changes a guy. For a few hours, he thinks to himself, 'Maybe I'm not so bad after all.' I'm sorry for tonight, Miranda. It was very selfish of me. I didn't consider how it would make you or anybody feel. I wanted you to like me because I wanted to feel wanted by someone like you. That's all."

Nora's gaze drops to her lap. Johm picks up his spoon and places it over the flame. Miranda stares at me through the dancing candle. In the delicate silence, she slowly lifts her glass of water and takes a sip without breaking her stare. She swallows, pats her lips with a napkin, and takes a deep breath.

"If you think this vulnerable sad-boy thing works because it's okay for men to cry now, I'm here to tell you that it doesn't," she says. "No one cares about your insecurities, least of all me. I understand you're trying to figure yourself out, but I've known capable, secure men before. They're on time, they have actual jobs, and they aren't so neurotic as to bring another woman on a date. No matter how progressive you think these times get, women will always want men who know themselves, so get that in your thick, boring head. Confessing your feelings is what's wrong with men. You don't want to fix yourselves; you want to justify yourselves. I came here because I wanted to give you a chance. I knew you were some bespeckled noodle-boy from the Midwest. But I'm sorry I looked past my assumptions. I have never been treated like this in my life. You're a self-loathing neurotic who will piss off every woman you know because you don't have a clue who you are. Thank you for this night. It was a great learning experience. You need to grow up. Goodnight and good luck, Peter Pan."

She takes another curt sip of water and pats her lips with a napkin, then she stands and slips her arms into a Burberry coat, adjusting her hair before buttoning it up. In moments like these, I never know where to look. Up? Down? There is nowhere to hide. One must face the humiliation of his own fiasco with open eyes.

"Goodnight, Miranda." Nora speaks up, unexpectedly.

It feels like the whole restaurant stops moving.

Nora's nose points at Miranda Maxwell like a cocked gun. "I'm glad you've decided who you are, because so have I. You're unkind, cruel, and ugly. You are going to find yourself an unkind, cruel, and ugly man who is very sure of who he is, and you're both going to live happily ever never. And when you're a forty-year-old WASP with kids

who hate you and a husband who cheats on you, you're
going to wonder why life didn't turn out as beautiful as it
did in the mirror. In that moment, you're going to remember this night and realize the cost of not being kind. Have a
good life."

She takes Johm's spoon away from the flame and places
it in front of him.

Amidst all her luxury and sense of security, Miranda Maxwell stands totally still, her fingers on a button of her coat,
staring at Nora in her robe and tennis shoes.

The waiter walks up.

"And here you go, ma'am, caviar with a wheel of brie.
Are we on one check this evening?"

The restaurant with the best ratings in Cambridge packs the
remains our artisan $70-a-plate dining experience in the same
white to-go boxes as any Chinese take-out. Johm swears the
six-dollar chocolate milk is Nesquik.

We return to the townhouse and plop onto the suede sofa
with an oversized wool blanket. The humiliation of the evening subsides. Nora warms up dino nuggies for Johm, and
we eat caviar while watching *Friends*, which Johm insisted
on, claiming Ross looks like his karate teacher.

He falls asleep after one episode.

"I'm sorry for such a lousy evening," I tell Nora.

"Take me to dinner and we're even." She takes a sip of wine. "She was a jerk. You don't want a girl like that."

"She was a pretty jerk."

"With pretty people, the jerk usually comes with it. It's a package deal."

"But you're pretty," I say.

"You think so?" This makes her frown, one cheek bulging with a caviar cracker. "I always thought my face was too long."

"No, I like your face. It's nice."

"Honest?"

"Honest."

The intro music to *Friends* plays, and it starts to rain. It is warm here, with Johm asleep in Nora's arms and Nora lying in mine, like clustering house cats.

"You've turned into quite the mother," I tell her.

She looks at Johm. "It's comforting to take care of someone else for a change."

"That's a good sign."

"Is it?" She turns to the TV. "I thought it was, but when the excitement of taking care of a child settles, it's the same thing all over again. I know I can do great things with my life, and yet I have no idea what I'm supposed to do, no idea how to unlock myself. A kid isn't going to save me any more than love will."

"It's not like that," I say. "I just think life is so miserable and full of grief and despair that falling in love is the best chance we have at fighting misery."

"Maybe," she says with tired eyes. "Would you like to hear my dream?"

"Yes."

"I had this dream that I worked for a company that didn't produce anything. There were hundreds of employees, but we only arranged meetings to schedule other meetings and wrote emails to each other. My boss calls me into his office and asks, 'Why are you here? What's life for? Why do we exist?' But like everybody else, I didn't have an answer. No one knows. But I had to give him an answer. I couldn't call in sick. Those are the rules of this dream. So, I presented him with money, two children, and tennis as a hobby. I said to him, 'Look, I don't have the answers, but you need an answer, and this is what I've got. This is it. Now will you leave me alone? Can I go watch *Friends* in peace?' He let me go, and on the train ride home, I met a monk, and I asked the monk if his boss ever bothered him with these questions, and the monk said, 'I don't have a boss. I'm self-employed.' Then I woke up."

The laugh track of *Friends* sounds like it's laughing at her dream. I heard somewhere that these laugh tracks are forty-some years old by the time they air, which means we're listening to the laughter of the dead.

Nora's head sinks onto my shoulder.

"I know what I'd show the boss," I say.

Nora slips into a sleep. The slow rhythm of their breathing is nice.

"This."

the story
behind
this story

(october)

9:16 a.m.

Hi Charlie,

This is your final warning to submit your short story for the first assignment. As you have been given two extensions, we will be unable to make any exceptions from this point forward.

Thanks, William

11:34 a.m.

Hi Professor,

Apologies for my delayed response, my grandmother caught COVID-19 and my cat, Chairman Meow, simultaneously committed suicide. As a result, I have been unable to focus on my academic responsibilities this past week, and for that I deeply apologize. I will get the assignment to you shortly.

Best Wishes, Charlie

11:50 a.m.

Hi Charlie,

I understand that family and pet emergencies come up. I happened to be at the Boston Bruins game last week and saw you came up in the "look-alike cam" so I assumed your situation was under control. Guess I was wrong. Please have your story submitted by tonight.

Best, William

12:12 p.m.

Hi Professor,

I have a perfectly good explanation for this. You see, my grandmother plays hockey—she's from Minnesota— and because one side effect of COVID-19 is death, she thought she was going to kick the bucket. As her last re-quest, she asked that I record the Boston Bruins game for her since they were facing the Minnesota Wild. As for my cat waterboarding himself in the sink, my parents called PETA and they are investigating the matter now.

They believe Chairman Meow suffered from a superiority complex (unrelated to his suicide). I will submit my story shortly.

Best Wishes, Charlie

12:18 p.m.

Hi Charlie,

I am sorry to hear about your cat. Because you were not present in class when students presented the context behind their writing experience, I will ask you to please write a brief email explaining why you wrote this story.

Thanks, William

8:03 p.m.

Hi Professor,

The context is simple. The evening of Chairman Meow's death, I sat in the Cabot House Common Room staring out the window, thinking of how my life could have been different. I recall when I was seventeen and going through an F. Scott Fitzgerald phase, I was interested in a girl named Elaine, but she was very pretty and had options. The rumor was she liked Lachlan, president of the robotics club, and me. I told her of my writing ambitions, and she asked to read something I wrote. I said I would write something and send it to her the following Saturday. She said she really anticipated my story. I wrote half of the story but never finished it. I don't know why I never finished it. I think I stopped writing because that's where I wanted our story to end—without an ending. She even asked for the thing on Saturday, but I lied and said my grandmother croaked from pneumonia and I never got around to writing it. She started dating Lachlan about two months later, and years later they are still together and happy. Or so I hear. The story I've attached below for this final is a finished version of the story I never sent her.

Best Wishes, Charlie

8:41 p.m.

Hi Charlie,

Thanks for your email. I'm afraid I'm having trouble with the validity of this backstory. The girl you claim to have known, Elaine, dates a man named Lachlan, but I find striking similarities between Lachlan McDrumond, inventor of the GamifyIt app, and his life partner Elaine Sans. The purpose of this academic exercise is not to create a fictional backstory but to explain the perspective you are coming from, interesting or not.

9:09 p.m.

Hi Professor,

I deeply apologize for the lack of clarity. No, this isn't made up. I'm afraid you are referring to the same Lachlan McDrumond, who was recently on the cover of *Forbes*'s "30 Under 30" issue. I never knew Lachlan in high school, but of course, I knew Elaine, the cocreator of the Gamifylt app—which I noticed *Forbes* failed to mention. Therefore, the context behind this story is that the first half was written back then, as a representation of how Elaine and I met and all, and the second half was written recently—an hour ago actually. It's the story I never finished. Admittedly, had I finished it back then, it might have a very different ending than the one now.

Best Wishes, Charlie

9:27 p.m.

Hi Charlie,

It looks like your attachment didn't come through. Please send again.

William

9:42 p.m.

Hi Professor,

I can't figure out how to attach the document, so I will copy and paste it. Thank you for a great start of the semester, I will rate you highly on RateMyProfessors.com.

Best Wishes, Charlie

9:43 p.m.

Charlie,

No, please don't copy and paste the whole thing into an email. I would prefer if you took the time to resolve any technical difficulties and send it as an attachment.

9:44 p.m.

Hi Professor,

No problem.

Best Wishes, Charlie

[copied and pasted from iPhone]

FUTURE NOSTALGIA

Warning: With your permission, I would like to tell you a story where nothing happens. This contains no plot, it is not funny, and there are no high stakes or burning desires in which all characters come out learning something. None of that. This is a story you'd tell a friend after the party is over, and it's late enough to tell any story you want without the burden of being interesting. It's just you and me.

There is a hotel in Cambridge on the side where people stay up late and talk casually about not-so-casual things. It is called the Charles Hotel, and hardly any person could walk away feeling undeserving of happiness. There was nothing to happiness in those days—it was just a matter of choosing where to be when it happened, on the beach with a crowd or alone in a quiet café talking to a star. I preferred the star, but the beach was also lovely. You could go anywhere and be at the right place.

On July 31, the last day for summer foreign exchange students, seven major flights got canceled in Boston due to an air traffic controller's strike. Rumor has it that the strike started when an influential air traffic controller fell in love with his boss, had an affair, but was quickly dumped due to his halitosis. This was not his fault—a new Subway employee accidentally put onions in his sandwich that day.

The broken-hearted air traffic controller took one public speaking class in high school, remembered most of it, and convinced his coworkers to strike, subsequently reconsidering a career in sales.

Hotels rapidly swelled to no vacancy, and anyone who got a hotel in Cambridge was cursed with luck. I was forced to get a room at the Harvard Square Hotel after some prankster set off all the sprinklers in my dorm.

As I lay in bed reading a book called *How to Be a Winner*, this fantastic song played outside near the train stations. It was Bob Dylan's "Simple Twist of Fate." I went downstairs to listen.

As I drew closer to the music, I saw the lights of the Charles Hotel from across the street. It gave off a sense of richness, but not money-rich—people-rich, something of a previous era, like a portal you could enter and leave anytime. I walked over to the Charles to investigate this feeling.

It was a gathering, and by the sound, it was no small affair. The entire hotel felt rowdy with foreign exchange students whose trips were interrupted by the strike. On the second floor, all the room doors were open. Jazz music blasted, and parties ignited out of nowhere. People went to and from each open room, sampling the alcohol. Boys and girls from all corners of the world descended on each other like a buffet. The Spaniards were falling in love with the Brazilians, the Italians with the Germans, and the Koreans with the Australians. An end to the summer, concluded with dancing, sexual boredom, and noise.

I sampled a few conversations but couldn't hear a thing

people said and forgot names instantly. You can never really hear anything at these parties. You're constantly saying, "What?"

In the near distance, I heard a voice. It sung past the noise and had a marvelous ring to it. The owner of this sharp soprano wore a flowing white summer dress. Dark curly hair outlined her tanned Grecian face, a face that told pages of stories, a face from centuries ago, something that didn't belong in this era or the next but perhaps arrived through an ancient gate. I could write on and on about her hazelnut eyes, so full of promise . . .

For a moment I was content just watching her while Paul McCartney's "Blackbird" played from some speaker.

I met a Londoner with a lisp, and he knew the circle of friends this girl was a part of. Remembering his Eton manners, he introduced me.

"Charlie, have you met so-and-so?" my new friend started. "This is Something Someone, this is Something or Another, and this is Elaine."

After we all weaved handshakes, Elaine spoke to me. She asked who I was and what I did to amuse myself.

"I don't know, I like to mess around with fiction," I said.

"What do you write about?"

"Human beings."

"Go on."

"Human beings doing human things that create human problems."

"Go on."

"We're all idiots, so I guess it's our mistakes that make us interesting."

She blinked in that charming way when you first meet somebody, a tongue-in-cheek way to say, "You're interesting, I like you," and that you want to play the game. *Sphallolalia*: flirtatious talk that leads nowhere.

"If I wrote a book, I'd never write an ending," she said.

"Why is that?"

"Well, if you're always beginning, you never have to say goodbye, do you?"

"I guess not. But that spoils the ending—the best part."

"Nah, who needs goodbyes anyway?" She brushed them away with a flick of her wrist.

I enjoyed the way her mind operated. I think she liked the attention people gave her. She thought out loud and didn't know what she was thinking until she spoke it, as if speaking to herself but also to the world.

"I'm bored! I'm so bored!" shouted one of the girls. "Let's hit the clubs."

Elaine gave me a wink and led two other girls and four men out the door. She turned and waved casually with her fingers.

"Goodbye." I waved back.

"Oh, it's not goodbye," she said. "It's hello."

There were many things to write about after midnight, whether it was a chess player shouting how he could feel his talent leaving him, or a young street artist painting a portrait while mumbling "*anche se mi uccide*," which I learned is Italian for "even if it kills me."

After Elaine and her group left to go clubbing, I thought she'd forgotten about me. That is, until I was listening to a street trumpeter playing "La Vie en Rose," and I spotted her alone, listening. Her dress flowed with the wind. I once heard that "La Vie en Rose," literally translated as "life in pink," means "life seen through happy lenses."

When Elaine saw me, she offered a suave, genuine grin. "Where have you been?" she asked.

"What do you mean?"

"I've been looking for an accidental run-in for the past hour now."

I liked the thought of her thinking of me. "Have tea with me," I said.

"Can you be a little more straightforward?"

"I really enjoy talking with you. This is fun, isn't it?" I asked.

"Right, you enjoy talking to me so badly you didn't follow me when we all went clubbing."

"I wanted to, but I don't like small crowds of strangers," I said. "Too much fake behavior."

"And what makes it real for you?"

"When you take out your inside thoughts and toss them to someone, knowing they won't drop them."

She said she liked that and would love to have tea with me.

We went into Tealuxe, a crowded tea café where no one can really hear you. I ordered us two coconut Earl Grey teas. A tenor sang Charles Aznavour's "She" around the street corner, its sound floating to our candlelit window table. In another corner, a couple argued with occasional self-aware glances. They would probably separate for the same reasons they got together, Elaine told me.

"You can't tell all that in one glance," I said.

"Maybe not every detail. But even if each person is different, we're all sort of the same, no matter who you are."

"Okay, go on." Now it was my turn with the *Go on.*

"At some point, we've all lost something, we've all loved someone, and we're all afraid of something."

"You're a romantic," I said.

"And you are?"

"Me? I identify as a postmodernist, quasi-pervert hypocrite myself."

She laughed at that. Every time she did, it brought

something new out of me. I laughed a lot with her. She could make me laugh forever if she wanted to.

"I'm romantic, but I know well enough not to expect the romantic stuff to last." She sipped her tea.

"Why not?"

"It just doesn't. History tells us that."

"Because people let it not last," I said. "It's people that's the problem."

"Well, no one's perfect."

We drank to that.

People with frowns walked by and we wondered what their lives were like, what they were suffering through and what the happiest parts of their day were. Some sounds and smells stay with us, reminding us in that unsaid whisper that we will remember this day many years later.

It was nearly 4:00 a.m. when we walked along the Charles River. We found ourselves on Weeks Bridge, staring at a tranquil Cambridge. Elaine's plane would leave in six hours.

"I have constant nostalgia for the future," she said out of nowhere. "It's when you experience a moment, and you know the moment will end, and you know you'll miss it, so you experience two kinds of longings—one now and one then."

"Is that what you're feeling now?"

She didn't answer.

"I think growing older, you realize something," she

continued, looking off into the water. "You think you will fall in love with many people. And the memories you look back on will be of only those few times you found someone to share your soul with."

"Everyone finds new people," I said. "In a way."

Then she turned to me. "The world is harder than we think."

"I know. And expensive."

"You might be bruised up a bit. You might not feel the same about life and all when it's through with you." She reached over and held my hand with her pinky finger. "You look at a picture, get a great feeling from it, and set it down, expecting to feel the same way in the morning. Sometimes you do, sometimes you don't."

That was a thinker, but when it hit me, it hit.

"Don't get lost, okay? Don't toss your insides to people who drop it," she said.

"If you say so."

"I do say so."

Elaine wanted to read my writing for some reason. I told her no, but she insisted, and I had a short story in my hotel.

I led her there, to the Harvard Square Hotel. We went upstairs, and I suggested she wait outside my door while I retrieved the manuscripts.

"Relax, Ted Bundy, I trust you." She walked right in, and I got this strange feeling that we'd known each other for years. She took a seat and offered a minibottle of Frangelico from her purse.

Outside, some guitarist played Nat King Cole's "Unforgettable." I handed Elaine a handful of beaten-up paper. I didn't tell her that just about every literary agent within a one-hundred-thousand-mile radius had rejected it. She lay on the bed and read each page. This was a nice break from the noise and heat—and for me, the crowd—to lay in a room, late, drinking with a long-lost friend from another life.

While Elaine read, I turned on the news. The flight delays had been resolved.

"Why do you write about escaping so much?" she asked after twenty minutes.

"You don't like it," I decided.

"No. Actually, I love it. I'm just curious."

"I come from a boring part of the country where all you have is your Bible and your imagination," I said.

"But you have so much more to write about. You don't see it because you're too busy escaping."

"I don't have a life, so sue me," I admitted. "I'm okay watching it all go by."

"What I'm saying is, you don't need to rely on imagination so much. Sometimes reality will do."

"Maybe it's just easier this way. It's easier to tell stories when you don't get too close. Instead of using that energy to participate, you use it later on, to make things up—maybe things you wish you'd done."

"That's how you write? With regret fuel?"

"Sometimes."

"I think you're afraid," she said.

"I am. Fiction over reality—no apology."

"Why?"

"Because reality will always break your heart," I said.

"So does fiction, the second you close the book."

Again, I went quiet.

"You want to hear something crazy?" she said. "In 1865, or whenever it was, a man on the train going from New York to Washington was returning home from Harvard for break. While waiting for his train on the platform, this young man fell onto the tracks. The train began to move. He would have died within seconds, but a stranger standing on the platform pulled him out by the collar and saved his life. The man who fell was Robert Todd Lincoln, son of Abraham Lincoln. The man who saved him was Edwin Booth, the older brother of John Wilkes Booth. Two months later, Edwin's brother would kill Robert Todd's father. If you wrote that, no one would believe you. They would say it's too contrived, too much. One day you're going to realize that reality is more fictional than fiction. The story is in the real stuff, Charlie. You don't have to make it all up. Just let it happen. Let it come to you."

She set the manuscript down and stretched, dancing to the window, pretending to look down on the streets. She turned and ruffled her hair. "So now the question is, do you and I kiss in fiction or reality?"

I don't think many people ever realize that it's the half-second details that make us fall in love—one glance, one chuckle, a flick of the hair. Half a second later, you go from Cary Grant to a dopey-eyed monkey. In that moment, that small moment no longer than half a second, Elaine occupied a place in me that no one had ever occupied before.

I walked over and touched her chin. I brought her face to mine. Her soft body melted into me. Time slowed. The rest of the world stopped and waited, watching, holding its breath and dropping its popcorn.

The sun peeked through the window and landed on her naked body, wrapped around sheets, resting on top of me. Her cheek lay on my chest. We secretly prayed for the sun to go back down and give us a few more moments.

But then it was time.

We got dressed and carried her bags to the lobby. Students scrambled with their luggage and Ubers and missed flights. We went through this war zone, and I found us a taxi. The driver was old and quiet and listened to old songs. Elaine and I held hands the whole time.

Logan Airport was, of course, a refugee zone. Elaine's flight was not full, though, so her line was sparse. Everything was confirmed, yet something inside me hoped something went wrong, delaying flights further. Nothing did. We sat near a coffee kiosk. The man running the kiosk played a song on his portable radio, Vera Lynn's "We'll Meet Again." I bought two cups of coffee and asked about the song. Many years ago, he told me, when he was in high school, he met a girl in New York who promised to meet him again one day. But on that promised day, she never arrived, and he became a normal man. But sometimes he played this song to remember the day she never came. Elaine and I listened, her face buried in my neck, as the song played on his speaker amidst the rabble. It was just us, and I wished forever to happen right then.

"I'll always remember you."

"I'll always remember you, too."

And then she flew away.

Most days are ordinary, like floating in the ocean with no wind. But some days are storms that take you places. You do nothing in particular. The wind takes you where it wants, to a place that makes all those other times not matter, and you let it.

There will always be people I miss. Everyone has them. You write about them, remember them, and finally leave them. No matter where they are in this too-big world of ours, I hope that on a sad day, out of nowhere, they'll remember me for a strange little moment, smile, and then go back to their odd little lives.

END

12:04 a.m.

Hi Charlie,

I read it twice. It needs substantial work. The prose is too ornate. Tell us the story simply, and in your voice. But overall, I appreciate you adapting this to the Cambridge environment. On an unrelated personal note, I sincerely wish you had sent her this story.

Best Wishes, William

12:21 p.m.

Hi Professor,

I know. I wish I did, too.

Best Wishes, Charlie

jumping out a window

(october)

It is two days before midterms, and students hide frowns under their beanies, pretending to be unconcerned but spilling their nervousness with fidgets of their pens. Snow arrived out of nowhere in the form of a winter storm the Weather Channel named Dick. Nora sneaked me into her dorm yesterday to let me sleep and study. I'm staying clear of Lamont and Widener libraries for a while until my situation blows over.

Last week, on a Wednesday, I met a terrific girl named Angie. The chemistry, the conversation, the spark—it was all there. I was riding cloud nine until we were sitting in an Indian restaurant and I told an unsavory joke about walruses. Evidently, Angie is fond of walruses. My joke hurt her, and she proceeded to vent these injured feelings to all her friends, including her boyfriend, whose existence I only learned about that day. Turns out, her boyfriend is the Harvard football team's prized tight end, Hank "Tank" Wilson.

Then I learned of a ridiculous "bounty" on my head: a one-hundred-dollar voucher to Insomnia Cookies. I thought it was a joke until a new hashtag went modestly viral:

#findtheglasseswearingtwerp

I guess Tank didn't like the idea of me emotionally abusing his girlfriend with walrus jokes. Apparently, he and Angie had this "open arrangement," but unfortunately he wasn't entirely on board with this progressive idea. He just didn't tell her how not on board he was.

I didn't think anyone would take this "bounty" thing seriously, being the twenty-first century and all, but, surprisingly, the reaction was somewhere in between. Acquaintances "joked" about the apparent drama between me, Tank, and his lover. "Funny, right?" And then, within literally fifteen minutes, Tank would conveniently appear.

The first time he teleported, I saw him, adjusted my glasses, and cleared my throat for a gentlemanly dialogue about the flawed passions of men. When I looked up, I saw a 230-pound Neanderthal charging. I learned then that I'm a naturally gifted long-distance runner. He chased me to MIT.

I continued to have faith that my academic sisters and brethren would stand by me, the wrongfully convicted man. This is the age of standing up for the underdog, the noodle-boy, the schlepper. From an outsider's perspective, they did. Online they denounced the harassment as bullying. But when I saw these Aldous Finches in person, they acted like they didn't know me. The plague of controversy had clung to my face. Not only was I being ignored, but the pattern continued: I go somewhere, someone recognizes me, Tank appears out of nowhere.

I know this sounds like something out of a '50s TV show, but I swear, this happened. Both the Harvard and Cambridge Police swore they'd "look into it" and proceeded not to grant me a restraining order. I no longer go to libraries, the Coop, the Science Center—nowhere is safe. Loyal friends have agreed to hide me. After six thirty, when it gets dark, I sneak into a dorm and hide from the storm troopers. Nora has been hiding me for three days now.

At 9:21 p.m., Nora and I munch on toast and quietly study in perpetual pajamas. Nora's room smells like lavender. While reading about groupthink, I realize that coffee and coffee-flavored water are the same thing. In that moment, I receive a phone call.

"Hello?"

"Charlie, what's happening?" It's Mike, and he knows exactly what is happening, that sonuvabitch.

"I'm studying in Leveret," I lie.

"Well, you'll never guess who I just met."

"You're probably right."

"Your future wife. I just shook the hands that will be running through your hair for the next two months."

"Thank you, Mike, I'm flattered you have faith that my wife and I will last two whole months."

"You've got to come over here," he sort of whispers.

"No. I'm a wanted man, dead or alive."

"But what is life without love? It's decaf coffee. There's no point."

"Chasing a girl is what got me into this mess."

"Spare me. Look, she said she knows you, but never had the guts to approach you."

"She knows me?" I wipe my glasses.

"That's what she said. You know what she told me?"

"What did she tell you, Mike?"

"She said, 'You know why I can't find the right man in Boston? Because they're all so modern. I want some boring nobody with grandpa vibes who can watch *Casablanca* with me.'"

"She did not say that."

"Look, she basically said that, okay? Now she really wants to meet you. Are you coming over or what?"

"Where are you?"

"Dunster House, the common room."

I say no and hang up. I can hear the snowy wind whistling

outside. Whether Mike is lying or not, that lonely whisper still finds its way to your ears on Saturday nights, saying, *What if this is it? What if this is the night you find what you're looking for?* Someone needs to do something about that whisper. It has brought me to many bad parties. I stretch, waiting for nothing, and then proceed to put my pants on. After all, aren't we all just waiting for the lottery?

Snow sprinkles down like donut sugar, making little "pit-pat" sounds outside Nora's foggy window. The smell of hot chocolate floats through her room. Dickens would be proud.

She phones up a friend and amateur makeup artist, Wilfred. Wilfred arrives and goes right to work disguising me with a fake unibrow and combing my hair into bangs like George Harrison.

"Just keep your face low," Nora advises with a stiff upper lip, helping draw the bridging brow, "and act a little weirder than usual so people avoid you."

"Weirder than usual?"

"Maybe have a limp. No one suspects anyone with a limp."

"Why am I weird?" I ask.

"And if anyone talks to you, pretend you're from Florida." She steps back to look at her work.

Wilfred stands behind her like a film director. "What about a mustache?" he asks.

"No, no, he must look like an idiot," Nora says. "I didn't have to do much, just a thing here and there."

"Am I actually weird?" I ask.

"Well, you think this'll do it?" Wilfred clicks his nails.

"Trust me," she says. "He's woman-proof."

"Woman-proof? Some girl wants to meet me, I can't look woman-proof—"

"If she likes you, you'll have nothing to worry about," Nora says.

"If people recognize you," Wilfred adds, "that's a lot to worry about, no?"

To complete their artistic vision, they put me in a black corduroy blazer with a wolf T-shirt underneath—one of those Walmart shirts with a thunderstorm and a high-definition wolf howling at the moon.

"Charlie." Nora holds my face like I'm going to war. "It is time. Be safe. We'll be here if . . . when . . . you get back."

I look at Wilfred. "We'll keep the kettle on for you," he says with a somber tone.

The downpour of snow keeps most eyes downward, so I am safe from being seen. "We Visited Harvard" postcards and calendars often feature pictures of the rowing team on the Charles River, near Weeks Bridge, and just behind it, Dunster House. The riverfront house is like Harvard's designated mascot.

I sneak into Dunster through the dining hall, passing lonely late-night diners. It smells like fish night. Colonial paintings and wood etchings hang on the walls of various corridors of mixed architecture, some colonial, some renovated modern. I make my way toward the common room where this event is taking place. The halls smell like an antique shop with a coat of fresh paint, like a new library full of old books.

No one recognizes me in passing, though I recognize some of them. I hear the commotion of a gathering in the common room. And music. I open the detailed double doors and feel the sudden swoosh of warm air hit my face. The entire party, it seems, is lit only by candlelight. Hundreds of long candlesticks scatter amongst a splatter of brass candleholders. The participants of this party are dressed in cardigans and turtlenecks and checkered skirts. Chet Baker's "Deep in a Dream" plays in one of those suitcase record players near the fireplace.

A semidrunk student in an unbuttoned vest tells me that this is some mixture of a poetry reading and group therapy. With only days before midterms, it should have been called "Procrastinator's Anonymous." Sprinkled throughout the room are crop circles of chairs with people reading their poetry to each other over "grape juice."

I glide to the fireplace, where four people encircle a tall man in a black suit sitting deep in a plush sofa with his penny loafers propped up on the coffee table. Mike.

He twirls the attention of his niche crowd with some story or pyramid scheme he managed to sell them. I don't recognize any of the three bored-looking girls sitting around the couch.

Sipping his "grape juice," he sees me and narrows his eyes, suddenly recognizing me through the disguise and lack of light. "The wayward son returns!" he yells with approval. "Why do you look like that?"

As he stands I grab his arm and pull him aside, hoping no one heard that last part.

"I'm in disguise," I whisper.

"As what, Dudley from Harry Potter?"

"Do I look that weird?"

"Don't worry, it suits you." He puts an arm around me and whispers, "This girl really wants to meet you. Her." He points his chin.

The person of interest possesses enormous jet-black hair, hoop earrings, and what looks like the prepackaged cliché attitude of a New Jersey housewife.

"Fellow humans, this is Charles," Mike announces. "Charles, meet fellow humans."

I receive halfhearted "heys" all around. A guy in a beret reaches over to shake my hand. "I'm Phillip."

"Nice to meet you, Phillip." His handshake is without grip or stability, a hand made of Jell-O.

Mike sits back in his spot. I'm on a separate sofa designed

for two, next to the Amy Winehouse imitator from Jersey. I don't recognize her from anywhere. Did we take a class together? She eyes me suspiciously, her legs crossed.

"Hello, I'm Charlie."

"Soph."

I lean on the arm of the sofa. We're not at the thigh-contact stage yet. We sit in silence. I look around the ceiling for something to stare at. She checks the condition of her elbows. The girl next to Mike says something about her dead grandmother, which he finds excessively funny, then quickly checks if he was supposed to laugh. Phillip is not entertaining his conversation partner in the slightest. It looks like he's selling her life insurance.

"So, have we met before?" I ask Soph.

"No." She adjusts the front of her dress.

"Are you sure?"

"Positive."

Maybe it's my disguise. "I'm Charlie."

"Soph."

I give Mike a look. He twitches at my gaze but rubs his chin, intentionally ignoring me. Very nice, Mike, well done. I offer to get the girl more "grape juice" and ask Mike for "a word."

He walks to the "juice bar" with me. "Mike, what the hell?"

"I know, isn't she smart? Getting her degree in brain surgery or something."

"She doesn't know me. What is this?"

He glances around to make sure no one is listening. "Look, the girls were giving me a hard time for not finding a friend for her. If I didn't come up with someone fast, they would have left."

"So, you came up with me?"

"I thought you'd like her."

"I'm leaving."

"No, wait!" He grabs my arm. "C'mon, don't be a shmuck, have a conversation. You'll have a great time. You know this isn't grape juice, right?"

"I'm not her type, and she's not mine."

"You've never dated anyone but your type. Seriously, look at the girls you've dated. They all look like they work at Star-bucks."

"Very clever, you should try stand-up."

"Seriously, Charlie, stop playing this movie in your head that you're going to meet your soulmate in some meadow. If you keep rejecting anyone that doesn't fit this perfect narra-tive, you'll always be alone."

"I'm fully expecting that."

"You're always attracted to people pretending they're a lot deeper than they actually are. It's like you're scared of confi-dent women because they might bring you back to reality."

He gathers a plate of olives with toothpicks.

"All right, fine," I say. "But I'm doing this for you."

"Well, I'm doing this for *you.*"

"I feel nauseous," I say. "I need an aspirin."

"You don't have to act confident. Be you. Be fine being scared."

"Mike, if I'm going to do this, you need to stop speaking in these beatnik riddles."

I down a cup of juice.

Okay, so I got off on the wrong foot, and now my nervous system is shot, but let me get my bearings. My game is strong, last time I checked. I've got this.

Mike returns to his seat, butt first, with a plate of olives for his dialogue partner.

"So, Soph," I start, this time sitting next to her on the sofa. She slow-blinks and gives me the "let's see what you got" face. "Have you heard that one about the mother walking with her son on the beach?"

She frowns.

"So, a mother is walking along the beach with her four-year-old boy when the surf comes up and sweeps him out to sea. He disappears. The mother drops to her knees and prays, 'Please, Lord, return my son, I beg you, I will live a good life from now on.' Suddenly the clouds open up, and a great beam of light shines right in front of the mother and deposits her son back to her. She picks him up, looks him over, then looks up at the sky and says, 'He had a hat!'"

Not even a grin out of Soph. I feel her sharp stare go straight through me.

"Really?" she says. "That's where you wanna start?"

Oh yes, New Jersey.

"Okay," I stretch my neck. "Do you like philosophy?"

"No."

"Do you have a brother?"

She frowns. "No."

I nod. She nods. We all nod.

"Well . . ." I break the silence. "If you had a brother, would he like philosophy?"

No one speaks after this. Yes, this is reality. I am actually trying to converse with this woman, and this is my line.

"That's an interesting haircut," she offers.

Then it hits me—my disguise. I'm not me. All past rejections that led to my disturbing lack of self-respect are lifted away, gone with the wind. I don't even exist anymore. I'm free from the neurosis, the ego, the cynicism, the internal gaps I thought could be filled with the fabled "hard work." Blessed with anonymity and a great apathy for consequence, any care of what others think or might think, what I think or ought to think, are all out the window. Adios. I'm someone else for the moment. A character in a video game; the protagonist of a lucid dream.

"Thank you, I cut it myself," I respond.

"You cut your own hair?"

"I do."

"You look in the mirror, and then you cut your own hair with scissors?" She really wants to clarify this.

"Well, you know, I figured if it works for Mark Zuckerberg, it works for me."

She forces a grin.

"So, you're studying for your master's?" I ask.

"I'm at the med school."

"Should we get coffee sometime?" I suggest.

"Do you know how many guys ask me out a week?" she challenges.

"Not enough?" I guess.

"Probably thirteen—per week."

"*Probably* thirteen?" I spot a weak point. "No 'probably' in 'thirteen.' It's either thirteen or it isn't. Someone's been counting."

We take a long sip from our cups, our eyes glaring at each other like cats about to fight. The grape-flavored courage juice doesn't taste nice when it's gulped like this, but its effects are working wonders on me. My face numbs slightly, and the nihilistic tendencies that translate into courage bloom.

"What do you usually do when a guy walks up to you, chatting you up?" I inquire genuinely.

"Depends."

"On whether he's good-looking or not?"

"Yes."

"What if he's not?"

"Then I brush him off, politely."

"Is that what you're doing here?"

"Yes."

"Then I'd better be persistent because I'd like to have much more than your number." Is that too much? That's too much.

"Like what?" She slow-blinks. Her dark eyes, thick with eyelashes, never leave mine.

"We can exchange conspiracy theories," I say. "I have a few about JFK. Then we can exchange life thoughts—you know, the special ones. Memories. Fears. I'd like to have your thoughts for a while, hold them until you feel understood, and then give them back to you in the morning. It's like an emotional lease."

She likes that; her eyes relax, like a drowsy smile. "Why do you want my ideas on how the world works?" She speaks with her hands. "Is it just because you think I'm pretty or something?"

"I didn't say you were."

"Oh, so I'm not?"

"Maybe you are. I don't know you too well. But compassion, now that's hot."

"You're so strange."

"So are you."

We stare intently, hating each other.

"Do you know why we're going to get along?" I ask. Our bodies are starting to lean toward each other, the way predatory birds do.

"Not a clue."

"Because we don't like each other. We're more honest with people we don't like than with people we do."

"That's not true at all."

"I'd bet my life it is."

"So, what, am I your 'type' then? Is that it?" Her hands get feisty.

"No. You're *not* my type—*that's* it." It looks like we're arguing. "Because you're *not* my type, what do I have to lose talking to you with no filter? Now that we sufficiently hate each other, we're going to show too much of ourselves, because we don't care. But if we liked each other, we'd try to hide our differences and flex our similarities. Ever notice you mirror the person you like? You find out they drink cashew milk, and suddenly your fridge is filled with that stuff. But that's the one way to really blow it with someone, by trying to make them stay."

"What, the more you try the more you fail?" she asks.

"Precisely."

"That's ridiculous. You're a kook."

"But not a phony."

"Oh, so I'm a phony?"

"Maybe. I don't know you. I've been a phony most my life and I'm lonely as hell. Maybe it wouldn't be so lonely out there if we faked a little less."

She clenches her jaw. "That's rude. You owe me an apology," she says.

"Accuracy hurts."

"Well, how about this for accurate: you're no Brad Pitt."

"You're no Meryl Streep."

"I hate you."

"I love you."

"You didn't just say that."

"I did."

And then she pinches my chin and kisses me. It is like a release of pressurized steam, a feisty, aggressive kiss. The kind that declares victory.

When she opens her eyes, the room, which had been still the whole time, begins shaking. Suddenly, I am Charlie again. Unsure, skinny, broke Charlie. My inner lemur wakes from its sedated sleep and loses its mind, swinging a grenade launcher into my neurons.

Soph stares at me, lips slightly parted. I can tell by the little throb in her neck veins that her pulse is also flying. But trying to stay cool, she keeps her nervousness hidden and manages a glimpse at my lips, and then my eyes, and then she lightly laughs, with a wrinkle in her nose.

This kills me. I run.

I run for the stairs without looking back and do not stop running for a good six stories. I could have kept running for six days.

I land myself in a common room with table tennis and billiards. There are no more floors to escape to. My wolf shirt is soaked. I collapse on a sofa and feel like dying. The sounds of two students ping-ponging away mimics a clock denting the pathetic silence.

I have never been so exhilarated in my life. I cannot believe this is reality. Somehow things will never be the same. What a human thing, to go years being one person and not knowing who this person is, but in minutes, recognize the force that changes us. The disguise gave me courage, but deep down, somewhere inside me, I was Charlie during that whole transaction.

I imagine times when I know God is mad at me for some religious joke I told. Sitting in this common room, staring at the three guys playing pool, I realize it is a "God's mad at Charlie" moment, because one of the three guys is Hank "Tank" Wilson.

Tank crouches down to take a shot, and directly above the pocket he aims for is my gaping mouth. He frowns his thick, freckled face at me.

"Do I know you?"

"Absolutely not," I say. His two friends turn around to inspect me.

"No, I swear, you look really familiar."

"I go to BU," I claim.

"What's your name?"

"Eugene. Everyone calls me Eugene."

His friends glance at each other, wondering if the name rings a bell.

"You play ball at BU or something?"

"No, I play squash." I get up quickly and try to escape casually to the elevator. "I dabble sometimes in water polo and watercolors, but only in the summertime when the Charles is warm."

"You play water polo in the Charles?"

"Yes. Yes, I do." I yawn, pressing the elevator button. "Well, it was good meeting you. I should head back, but this was great fun. Let's do it again sometime."

"Yeah, sure." Tank goes back to his game.

The elevator door opens and Tank's girlfriend, Angie, steps out in yoga pants.

"Charlie! Oh my God, wow, it's so good to see you!"

She gives me an unrequited hug. Of all people to instantly recognize me through my disguise, it's her. I guess she's over the walrus joke. "I've missed you. Where've you been? I love your shirt."

"Oh, you know how it is, exams, water polo . . ." I enter the elevator and press the first floor till my finger hurts. Tank and his trio glide over like Dobermans, billiard poles in hand. "I got a new boyfriend!" I say, as loud as I can. "I've got a new boyfriend, and oh he's just a peach."

The elevator isn't closing.

"Really?" Angie frowns. "I had no idea you were . . . I mean I thought after we, you know—"

"Talked? That night we just talked? Yeah, talked." I look at Tank for affirmation. "Well, actually, that's when I knew I was into guys."

"Oh." Angie seems shocked by this. "Right. Did you get a new haircut or something?"

"Say, babe, I'm going to get a drink downstairs. Just wait here." Tank looks at me when he says this.

"Get me one of those frosted pretzels, will you? Make sure it's fat-free."

Tank is already in the elevator when he grunts that he will. He towers over me. I can see which chest hairs are ingrown. The doors close. I watch the light fade. In just four stories, I will be turned into a quadriplegic.

Suddenly, a hand stops the elevator from closing. Two skinny men wearing incredibly tight matching jeans enter the elevator, talking office politics.

"Well, you know Sara's just a bitch about changing the cyan ink cartridge," one says.

"Isn't she? I mean, it's not even half empty before she's blaming me."

The doors close.

"Get this, I'm at CVS last night, and I run into her. She says, 'Did you change the cyan cartridge at the labs today?' No 'hello,' no 'hey, how's your day'—nothing."

"Un . . . be . . . lievable."

More silence. The elevator squeaks.

"Look, Tank, it's a mix-up," I start. "Nothing happened with me and Angie."

"The hell nothing happened. You call ice-skating and going to a movie 'nothing'?"

"We saw a rerun of *Cats*. It was so bad it shouldn't even count!"

"Shut up."

"She didn't mention you. She acted like she couldn't pronounce 'boyfriend.'"

The tight-pantsed sophomores glance at us. I don't think they'll ever know they just saved my life. If I ever have children, they'll have to thank these two.

"Listen, I do have a boyfriend," I promise.

"Yeah, sure you do."

"Meet him; he's downstairs right now."

"Where?"

"In the common room."

The elevator arrives and the doors open. Tank grips my arm. "Show me."

I take him to where the party is. A crowd of people might save me, though it's unlikely. Tank is very popular, and most people don't have the courage to yell wolf.

"Stay cool," he whispers right before the door. "You yell once, I'll break your fingers."

The gathering is winding down. I can feel the initial excitement and social pressure to appear likable has vanished. The snacks have not been refilled at the table. Tank isn't joking about the fingers. He wrenches hold of mine, so we walk together, hand in hand, one happy couple.

We make a full circle around the room, receiving odd looks from people.

"He's not here, is he?" Tank sneers.

"He was just here," I whisper back, looking for Mike.

"Let's get out of here."

"Wait!" I stop him.

I see Soph chatting up a tall, gawky-looking character by the fireplace.

"There she is." I point with my nose. "That's my girl-friend."

"I thought you said you were into guys."

"Well, I go back and forth a lot. I'm in that free-trial period you know?" I stammer. "She doesn't know about him, and he doesn't know about her. Who loses?"

Tank is not amused.

We walk over, nice and easy. When Soph sees me, she looks like she fell off a bike. Horrified, mystified, and ever so slightly glad I came back.

"You're back." Her dark eyebrows rise with a look of in-terest, the look when you receive a compliment.

"Why, naturally, moon pie," I say.

"I'm not your moon pie."

"Of course you aren't." I look at Tank and whisper, "She's not my moon pie."

"What do you want?" She's probably wondering why Tank and I are holding hands.

"I want you to meet this gentleman. He plays on the Harvard football team. Tank is the tight end."

"Hi." She looks unimpressed.

The three of us stand in silence, grinding our teeth.

I start again. "Say, honey—"

"Don't call me honey," she says.

"You got it. Do you remember the time we first met?"

She lets out a mocking laugh through her nose.

"How I said I loved you, and you said you hated me, and how I kissed you right then and there?"

"Oh, you kissed me, yes." A curl forms in the corner of her mouth.

"Now, tell me, honestly, did you think I was good-looking or what?" I ask.

"Let me put it this way," she banters, "I thought Spock and John Lennon had a baby. But you had a lot of nerve calling me out. Pretty impressive for a first date."

"Why, darling, I didn't even know it was a date."

She smirks. "You're strange."

"So are you."

"I hate you."

"I love you."

She laughs a wonderful husky laugh, and my inner lemur does a celebratory backflip as I look to Tank for approval.

"All right. I'll go on a date with you," she says.

"What do you mean, you'll go on a date with him?" Tank inquires.

"Well, what do you want me to say, we'll try this thing for a year?"

"Wait a minute." Tank sticks out his giant hand. "You're not his girlfriend?"

She looks at me.

"You told him I was your girlfriend? We just met about five minutes ago, you weirdo."

Well, I'm certainly a dead man now. Tank looks delighted about the new circumstances.

I bite his arm. He curses, and I shove him onto a table of cheese. I run for it, back up the stairs. Tank is behind me, sprinting like a lion, with traces of provolone in his hair. On my way up, a student carefully maneuvers his way down the stairs with a swivel chair. He graciously accepts my offer to give him a hand, and I heave the chair down into Tank's path. This buys me time.

I burst into the sixth-floor common room, where Angie sits on the sofa reading *the Harvard Gazette*.

"Hi, Charlie."

I sprint past her to the window and open it, gazing at the six stories that end in snow. Jason Bourne fell twenty stories and survived. I know six can be done.

Before I jump, I hear behind me, "Babe, did you get the fat-free pretzels?"

I discover something serene about being in midair. Everything slows, each snowflake pausing, every noise fading. Time transcends into ice, melts, and becomes ice again. As I float through the first second, approximately six babies are born, three people die, two couples marry, Dunkin Donuts sells twenty cups of coffee, and Warren Buffett earns four hundred bucks. By the time I hit the ground, these numbers double.

I land on a snowman.

I lie there in the snow, thinking about my life.

About twenty feet away stands the woman named Soph, who is not my Moon Pie, midway through putting on her coat. Her eyes are like a taxidermized deer.

We consider each other, wondering whether this is a dream. About thirty babies and ten marriages later, the reality is clear.

"I forgot to ask for your number," I say.

Her lips ask if I am crazy.

"I don't know," I reply.

"You have issues."

"Well . . ." I find the snowman's nose, a carrot, and bite into it. "The thing is, you're either crazy or everybody else is."

"Are you okay?" She comes over and pokes my arm.

In truth, I'm fine, but I tell her I can't feel my liver. She says she'll call an ambulance.

"No, it's fine, it's just—" I wince, to make it more convincing. "If you could just help me up, I should be all right."

I suggest that I rest and get some tea because everything is better with tea. Soph pulls me out of the snowy rubble and slinks my arm across her shoulder. The snow is still coming down, pitting and patting like a million tiny people walking in and out of each other's little lives. She smells like rose extract. Her shoulder is sturdy, trudging on in the cold, pulling a *Saving Private Ryan* in heels.

"I've got to say," she says as we hobble across the empty Old Yard. Tank is not behind us—no one is. We're in the clear. "I've never felt so safe in a conversation with a stranger. We were talking, and suddenly it felt like I'd known you for years. Like we'd been through a whole relationship in the matter of five minutes."

"It was three minutes, my Moon Pie."

"I'm not your Moon Pie. It was five."

"Three."

"Five."

"I jumped out a window for you. It was three."

She laughs at this, and we limp slowly on, into our first accidental date.

the vent

(november)

My romantic low from the beginning of the semester descends into a nosedive by November. Soph, a woman I had a brief thing with—maybe five or six things with—earlier in October, during that surprise snowstorm, stopped calling. Our fling showed all the signs of a long-lasting relationship: she is older by six years, studying to become a literal brain surgeon at Harvard Med School. Comparably, my summer internship application at *Dr. Phil* was rejected. My last-ditch attempt to save this doomed fling is through a song I've memorized. I don't sing, but here I am, so I guess she's worth it. It is her favorite jazz tune from Chet Baker, "I Fall in Love Too Easily."

"I still think it's in C minor." Ted sits behind the Fazoli grand piano, holding the C minor chord like the Close button in an elevator. We wait in the Adam House common room for Mike to come down. The fireplace emits dancing shadows. "You ask me, I think she's over you," he says casually.

"We don't know that," I say. "It could be a maybe."

"Maybe means no."

"Maybe means maybe."

"No means no. Maybe means no. Yes means maybe."

"Just play the song, will you?"

I put the phone on speaker, and it purrs the ringtone. No answer. Ted scratches his nose and winces after the fifth ring.

"Hello?"

I look at Ted. This is it. "Soph?"

"Hi, Charlie." She sounds tired.

"You sound lovely, how are you?"

"I smell like raw brains and I'm tired."

I glance at Ted for analysis. He shrugs. "Well hey, Soph, I have a surprise for you."

"Charlie . . ."

"I'm not sure how the piano will sound across the phone, but here it goes."

"Charlie . . ."

I signal to Ted, who tinkles out the introduction. I sing: "I fall in love too easily—"

"Charlie, I'm engaged."

Ted stops on a low D note, looking like he's just seen a naked man. The fireplace pops.

"Right . . ." I try to sound casual. "Well, have you picked a date?"

"I was always engaged. Sorry I didn't call you sooner."

My heart beats twice the rate of the grandfather clock, waiting to hear something different, ideally something like *Never mind, actually I want you, a twenty-year-old noodle-boy.* Brains go through bizarre scenarios to avoid the hurt.

After a long beat of silence, Soph says, "Goodbye, Charlie," and the three-note *boop-boop-boop* sound on FaceTime echoes traumatically.

"Whoa." Ted seems genuinely fascinated.

I fall into the sofa. "I learned that whole stupid song for nothing."

"Yeah. You did."

"Why is life so full of rejection?"

Ted blinks. "I don't know. Evolution?"

He does have a point, and regardless, that's a perfect breakup line: "Look, nothing personal baby, it's just evolution."

I wish—perhaps that was my first mistake—that the brain cramp called consciousness could be shiatsu massaged until it was no longer sore to think. We walk into one heartbreak after another throughout our lifetimes. Maybe that is the whole point.

Ted and I wait outside Adams House for Mike to come down. He is upstairs preparing for his date, no doubt dabbing cologne in forbidden places. What an optimist.

I leave my phone. The sight of it is temporarily depressing.

Ted tries consoling me—I guess that's in the "friend" job description. He theorizes that she probably thought I was an incompetent boy with no money.

At 6:33 p.m., the door opens, and Mike steps out in a 1960s-style burgundy suit and black tie. He looks like a Jersey Boy.

"Gents, get ready." He flashes us a Norman Rockwell grin.

"That girl just broke up with Charlie," Ted blabs.

"What girl?"

"Nothing," I say.

"Oh, that brain surgeon? The one ten years older than you?"

"Six years, and yes, the brain surgery *student*," I clarify, "that you introduced me to, thank you very much. But don't worry about that. I'm over it. I'll go see a movie or something."

"Did you sing her that Chet Baker song?"

"No."

"That's rough, sorry. You were practicing for weeks."

"Yes, yes I was."

"All for nothing," Ted adds.

"Thank you, Ted."

"I feel good." Mike eyes himself in a round mirror. "You know that feeling when you're at the beginning of something, and you have all this energy because you know everything will be okay?"

"No."

We walk down Brattle Street, where he is supposed to meet his date. I've never seen him so optimistic.

"Hey, when you see her, don't mention I wanted you guys to meet her, yeah?" Mike says.

"Why not?" Teds asks.

"Trust me, just say I bumped into you guys."

"You bumped into us?" I repeat. "Sure."

"Did Charlie and I bump into each other first, and together we bumped into you, or did we simultaneously bump into you?" Ted clarifies.

"Sure, whatever, say we all bumped into each other."

"But why would we bump into each other, then go the same direction for five minutes, only to turn around and go a different direction?"

"Ted, I don't know, make something up."

"I like the simultaneous bumping idea," I say.

"Guys, just pick a story—"

Before Mike can finish his command, a girl in a beige parka and black tights waves just ahead of us, from in front of Burdick Chocolates. Accidentally, we all wave back in unison.

"Hey," Mike croons as we approach her. "How are you?"

She emits a faint smile with distractingly white teeth and goes in for the casual hug. "Good! Just busy."

"These are my pals, Ted and Charlie." Mike turns to us. "I bumped into them."

"We bumped into each other," Ted robotically clarifies. "Separately. You see, we all casually bumped into each other, and upon bumping we decided to take a brief, platonic stroll."

"Oh . . ." The girl tilts her head back at this fascinating backstory.

"Anyway . . ." Mike turns to us with a stern expression. "I'll see you guys later."

"It's nice to meet you." I shake her mitten-wearing hand, and Ted gives her a high-five.

Ted and I accidentally walk in the same direction as Mike and his date. We slow down, hoping they pass us, but they linger, hoping to create distance. When Ted and I realize this, we start speedwalking, just as Mike and his date pick up the pace, hoping to pass us. We turn the corner on Story Street and lose them.

As Ted and I pass the post office on Mt. Auburn, I see a woman just ahead. She kneels over a large vent in front of the bus garages, and whenever a bus comes rolling out, she runs to the sidewalk and then returns like a sandpiper.

She cross-bends her legs, flight-attendant style, apparently searching for some lost thing worth getting run over for. Her hair is damp, like she's been running. When she retreats a fourth time to the sidewalk where we stand, she notices us and brushes strands of her blond hair off her forehead. She looks somewhere in her midthirties, with a worried, piercing face and opal eyes, the kind of beauty that demands two beats before moving on. She wears a black, plunging dress, with pearls and high heels and a coat with fur lining. I don't know fashion, but I know her income level is clearly out of place near the buses.

"Can we help?" I offer.

She points to the vents and says something that sounds like Russian.

"What's down there?" I ask.

She says more in Russian, pointing at the vent.

"Sorry, I don't understand," I say, gesturing.

Her hands summon us. "Come," she says with a hard *k* sound. "*Come.*"

From Ted's stoic expression, I assume he is caught in the headlights by her irrefutably sensuous aura.

We stand over the vents, and warm steam sprouts up, filling our clothes and relieving us from the cold. The strange Russian kneels down and wriggles this rusted metal ring wrapped around the bars of the vent. As the headlights of a bus find us, like escaped prisoners we run back to the sidewalk, cold from the sudden contrast. I shiver.

The woman speaks more Russian and gesticulates what looks like a heart.

"You dropped your . . . heart in there?" I turn to Ted. "Maybe she dropped her wedding ring."

"Yes," he says with a starstruck expression. "I *also* noticed she isn't wearing one."

The bus passes, and she leads us back to the warmth. I kneel down to take a better look. It seems she is pointing at a rusted padlock.

Ted attempts to use his phone as a flashlight, but his battery is dead.

"Do you have the key? The *key*." I gesture.

She shakes her head, "*Nyet, nyet . . .*"

The padlock isn't made of steel, but it's also not tin. It could have been used for a flimsy high school locker. An inscription is etched on the surface: *Tatiana & Mikhail, 2003*. I recognize it as a love padlock, the kind you see on chain-link fences to symbolize cheap infinity. Maybe that's why she wants it. Because it doesn't mean nothing to her.

My clothes are damp from the steam and my body shivers. I leave Ted and the stepmother of his dreams in communication chaos. I'm sure he's happy just to hear her voice. I jog to CVS, three blocks away, and buy a five-dollar Phillips-head screwdriver. The cashier's name is "Ok," and I tell him how much I appreciate his name.

"Okay," he says.

When I jog back, Ted still believes he can break through the language barrier.

"Man, love. Am I right?" he tells her. "Love really ought to have a catch to it, like a love tax or something."

She smiles and frowns at the same time.

"'Cause, you know, all good things have a catch to them." He laughs, and she laughs because he laughs.

"There is a catch to it, Ted." Kneeled down, I insert the screwdriver into the ring portion of the padlock. "It ends." I hold the lock with one hand and twist the screwdriver with the other, using leverage to bend the metallic ring. My muscles shake until I feel a sudden pop.

"You broke it?" Ted yells.

"I hope she kept the warranty back in 2003."

The damp padlock swivels from the hinges, and I give it to her as another bus approaches and we run to the sidewalk.

She is overjoyed, and for a moment, amidst the self-babbling, I could swear she is on the verge of tears. She plants a soft kiss on both our cheeks. Ted's lips tighten.

"Well, goodnight." I put up my hand.

"*Nyet*," she exclaims, already walking. "*Pojdemte*—come, come."

I recognize something poetically seductive about this, the danger of a strange older woman from a different land come-hithering two Americans to go somewhere far, far away, where all things are good and beef jerky prices are half off.

Ted looks like he's been told he's going to Disneyland.

"Oh, absolutely I will," he whispers.

"*Pojdemte*," she keeps saying.

We obey our marching orders, and she smirks at her powers of persuasion. I'm assuming this goes down one of two ways: either we're idiots for following her, or we're idiots for not following her. I don't know the rules, but when a beautiful woman says "Come," you come.

Her heels tap the sidewalk of Hillard Street, the way they do in noir movies where the mysterious blond seems all right until she pulls a tiny gun from her garter belt in Act Three. But Humphrey Bogart always smacks her in the jaw before she pulls the trigger, so all clichés being equal, maybe Ted and I are in good hands. Then again, we're no Humphrey Bogarts, and at 6'6" in heels, she can easily take us both.

On Garden Street, a little past the graveyard and beyond the Unitarian church that offers terrific lemon bars on Sundays, guests walk in and out of the Commander Hotel. Our Russian enters without looking to see if we're behind her. The doorman's eyes stoically twitch down to our shoes and up to our heads, not reserving judgment. She leads us through the lobby that smells of coffee. Green shrubbery surrounds us like a forest. We've entered her territory now. A little beyond the lobby, she walks us through an empty ballroom.

"Charlie," Ted whispers. "Let's set some ground rules. No looking down."

"Jesus Christ, Ted."

"I'm serious." Yes, he really is. "When we get to—where I think we're going, neither of us looks at the others' . . ."

Before I can answer, we enter another door, this time to a hallway. Two men in black leather jackets stand at the end. Ted glances at me. By now, sounds of the lobby muffle to a distant hum. Our mystery woman casually mutters something in Russian to the men in black leather jackets and they let us through a set of double doors that open to a ballroom, like the one before, but this one has at least four hundred people in suits and ball gowns. The men are ugly, and the women are beautiful. No music, only chattering, all in Russian. A microphone and grand piano sit unused in the middle of the room. Outside is a cold and lonely Cambridge, and here, not even a mile away from Harvard Yard, through a few anonymous grand hallways, is mini St. Petersburg. Ted and I are certainly outside our habitat now. We help one stranger, and suddenly we've entered the Russian *Great Gatsby*.

Our leading lady takes us to a table where a balding man in his late sixties sits. Just by his stillness, his seeming immunity to any kind of stimulant, I know he's rich. His glasses rest on the bridge of his crooked nose as he scrolls through something on his phone without much movement beyond his thumbs. Four bored men in black suits surround him at nearby tables. One of the suits routinely stands, giving me the up-and-down. The mystery woman comes around and kisses this Vladimir Gatsby on the cheek. His eyes follow her, but his face remains still. I think it is safe to say that Ted and I will not be entering an *Eyes Wide Shut* party tonight.

She murmurs something to the boss man and shows him the broken padlock. His eyes flicker between the padlock and us. After a minute's worth of her innocent-seeming explanation and his sinister stationary listening, our mystery woman blows us a flirtatious kiss and saunters off to another table, leaving us to our fate. He allows us to approach with a subdued nod. We walk to his table and sit, not sure if we're allowed to.

Silence. He stares at his phone. Something isn't right; I had a bad feeling when I saw him, now I have a terrible feeling.

"Men without women," he begins with a thick Russian accent. "Like boots without socks, no?"

Ted and I stay silent.

"But men *with* women . . ." His eyes never rise from his phone. "Like two feet in one boot."

"Women, am I right?" Ted thinks this comment is productive.

More silence.

"So, what happened to the music?" I try to stir something up.

"They let me down. Do you know why you are both here?" he asks.

My toes curl. Intuitively I say, "We'll have to get back with you on that. She didn't really tell us where we were going."

The man's fingers stop moving on his phone. He finally looks up. His shark-gaze at Ted seems meaningless until I notice what he's staring at—the red kiss mark on Ted's left cheek.

"She says you were both very helpful."

"It was nothing," I remark.

"You say it was nothing, but it makes her happy to recover her toy." He pokes at the padlock. "She tells me to reward you both."

"Oh, really, no need."

"She leaves the premises by herself without security." He pulls a checkbook from his coat. "This little trinket must mean so much to her, no?"

"It's a love lock," I say, as if he couldn't tell. "Tatiana and Mikhail. She must be Tatiana, then?"

His face remains stoic.

"And you must be Mikhail."

He shakes his head.

"Oh, I see." My back gets sweaty.

He nods, slowly.

"Mikhail Popov, political science, Harvard University class of 2004. Why do I know that?" he asks.

"You looked it up?" Ted offers.

The man's mouth grins, but his eyes don't follow. "Women talk of their past like men talk of sport trophies." He tears off the check with his middle and index finger and holds it like tissue. "When I was eight, I wanted a rifle. My parents asked me why, and I said to shoot an owl that kept me awake at night. They said I was not to bother the owl. It was bad luck. But that month, in a wrestling match, I won a slingshot. Every day at three forty-five p.m., I would practice my aim with the slingshot until I could hit pine cones in tall trees. On the ninth day, my father beat me. Why, you ask? I didn't kill the owl. I didn't even try. But an act without intent is a crime against others. Intent without the act is still a crime against you. My father beat me, for me. It takes many years for a man to realize that his punishment is a present."

He flicks the check across the table, and it flutters down in front of me. I glance at the number: $800. He mutters something in Russian to the four men in suits and they stand, yawning.

"You don't know why you are here, and yet you follow a strange woman to a hotel." His eyes go back to his phone. "And so, gentlemen, this is my present to you. It will be over quick if you don't resist. If you put up a fuss, they will break your fingers. Goodnight."

Four men in suits are now standing behind us. One politely gestures at Ted to stand up. I thought people only get beat up in movies. I pray for this to be a dream and that I'm going to wake up soon and be grateful for my life again.

"Wait, I think there's been a misunderstanding," I say.

Before I can say more, a Dolph Lundgren–type bodyguard slides my chair back, dragging all 140 pounds of me as easily as pulling out sheets.

"Hello, my name is Luka." He shakes my hand as I stand. "I will be beating you up this evening."

"Oh my God."

"Do not worry," Luka explains. "We will beat you up fair."

"Fair? What does that mean?"

"Oh, you know, we don't break anything, we don't hit the nose, the stomach, or the eyes—"

"No, no, we can go for the stomach," one of the bodyguards interjects.

"No, you shouldn't, you can really hurt someone like that," says Luka.

"Yeah, you can," I agree.

"It's what happened to Harry Houdini," Ted adds.

"Houdini, there we go," I repeat.

The discussion turns Russian. They whisper as if it were

private. Ted cautiously pulls out his dead phone again, trying to turn it on. Nothing.

"So, here's the situation." Luka turns to me. "Pavel over there says he's never hit a man with glasses before, and he wants to know if he can try it on you."

Pavel gives me a warm grin.

"No." I straighten my glasses. "You said no eyes; the glasses count as eyes."

"Yes, but it's his birthday, and he was wondering if you could make an exception."

"No, absolutely not. Happy birthday, but these are my eyes."

"Pavel's had a tough year, with his girlfriend leaving him and all," Luka explains. "It would really mean a lot to him."

"I understand that, I really do," I say, "but my optometrist moved to Nashville last year to pursue songwriting, and he made these frames custom. So, no."

Luka explains this to a visibly disappointed Pavel.

"Look, can he settle for a sock in the jaw or something?" I ask.

Luka converses with Pavel, and after a moment, he turns back to me.

"He said he's tired of jaws. He wants to try something new this year."

I rub my temples. "I can't think right now, everything's happening all at once."

After a volley of words, the four bodyguards put something to a vote—two raise their hands. I raise my hand, too, but my vote isn't counted.

In the commotion of choosing our doom, I nudge Ted's foot. Swallowing once, his head faintly motions agreement. We casually turn and walk toward the nearest cluster of bodies. My heart is beating a million miles an hour. We make it ten steps before the bodyguards notice. They instantly follow, but they remain calm. No need to panic anyone at the party.

"Do you see any other exits?" Ted whispers, repeatedly trying to turn on his dead phone.

"Just don't let them get ahold of you," I say.

"Let's yell that we're in danger."

"Ted, I have a feeling these guys are serious about breaking fingers."

The black suits spread out and flank us, closing in. A few people glance, noticing, but make no effort beyond that. We are a few large strides away from the piano and microphone.

"Ted, play something on the piano." I take his arm and beeline for the Steinway.

"What?"

"Play 'I Fall in Love Too Easily.'"

"What key was it in again?"

"E♭ minor."

"I still think it's in C minor."

"Ted, you play this thing right now or we're dead."

I throw him on the piano seat, and he instantly fingers some lounge-room chords. I tap the microphone three times. The room bubbles down. Guests toss their chins at us. The bodyguards disperse, in a conundrum now that we have mustered some attention, but they continue to surround us from a distance, lingering like sharks.

"Good evening, ladies and gentlemen, you . . . cool cats and kittens." Nobody gets this reference, but I try to lighten them up a bit more. "I heard a good one the other day. A lawyer, a blond, and the pope walk into a bar. The bartender says, 'What is this, some kind of joke?'"

Not even a sigh. Russians. "Well, anyway, you guys like jazz?"

The bodyguards glance at each other. No one seems in charge. I give Ted the nod. He transitions from the lounge-room chords into the song.

I start to sing: "I fall in love too easily . . ."

The guests seem to like this, contributing their expensive attention. Ted hides his nervous mess-ups in minor chords. We've practiced this number for weeks. We've never played

this well in our lives, and, coincidentally, we are playing for
our lives.

An elderly woman with a feather in her hair loves our act.
She sways to the song, alone. As we sing the third chorus, I
notice that Luka keeps looking back at the big boss, still at
his table. The big boss looks up and notices us with a blank
face but returns to his work.

The song ends. The guests applaud. Pavel, the one who
wants to end my glasses, is standing by the door.

"I believe it's someone's birthday today," I blurt out.
"Ladies and gentlemen, raise your glasses for Pavel!"

I point at Pavel. The guests don't care, but now that we
have their attention, they're willing to play along.

"Raise your glasses for Pavel!" I walk toward Pavel.

Ted follows, singing: "Happy birthday to you . . ."

Three guests quietly mumble-sing. Then eight. Then the
whole room is uncomfortably singing a monotone "Happy
Birthday" in Russian.

Pavel shifts his weight, confused and serious, uncomfortable with the attention. I slap him on the shoulders, singing,
and by the third verse, Ted and I are wading toward the door.
The other bodyguards do some wading of their own, gliding
through to block our escape.

When I hear the last "to . . . you . . ." in Russian, we
open the door and sprint. The security guard manning the

doors yells something. Probably Russian for "hey," but I don't want to ask.

We reach the lobby, panting. Luka, Pavel, and the other guards follow. But now it's a home game, because four grown men in matching black suits is a very odd sight in today's society. Especially in a hotel lobby. They get plenty of stares. People must think they're a boy band. I go to the front desk.

"Excuse me," I say. A girl named Kit helms the front desk. She gives us the up-and-down.

"We're in room one-two-three, and it seems we are getting harassed by those gentlemen over there." I theatrically point at the Backstreet Comrades. They see this and turn their backs.

"What seems to be the problem?" Ms. Kit is skeptical.

"Well, they claim they are members of the Westboro Baptist Church, and they keep following us and asking if we would like to be saved."

"Oh, I see." Ms. Kit now senses the gravity of the situation. When Luka and his boys see her pick up the phone, they return the way they came. "Let me call security."

"Thank you," Ted says. "So how long have you been working here?"

I grab his elbow and fast-walk out of the lobby.

Our skin is damp from the run, and the crisp Cambridge air bites. We book it down Garden Street and past the graveyard until we are back in Harvard Square. I've never been more grateful for all five fingers. I feel like crying, and Ted is already crying.

We sit at Dunkin' Donuts, processing our night.

"It's like the story of Joseph, isn't it?" Ted says over a blueberry donut.

"What is?"

"Remember that scene in the Bible where Joseph gets hustled by a hooker, but she's not his type, so she gets mad and rats him out to her boyfriend?"

"Yes."

"Well, it's kind of what happened tonight, with us, isn't it?"

I don't have the energy to argue allegories, so I just agree. My back aches with tension. I think of Soph, oddly enough. In hindsight, my eviction from her life was inevitable. But perhaps our evolutionary design is to give the burden of being left alone to the one who can take it. At least I hope it is. In the short time I knew her, I learned her life had been a hurricane of abandonment, debt, and internal chaos, and maybe if I left her, it would have done her in. It's like the last gift you give to someone you love: you take on the weight of being alone so they don't have to.

"Is that Mike?" Ted points out the window. Coming out of Toscano, an Italian restaurant with forty-dollar linguine, Mike and his date step out into the cold. They face each other, hands in pockets. After a moment, they wave, and she walks away. Mike pretends to tie his shoelace as he watches her disappear.

Ted steps out of Dunkin' and waves. "Say, Mike! We have donuts."

Mike comes inside, scarf still on. His lips are thin.

Ted sits back down and gulps a coffee. "How'd it go?"

"I don't want to talk about it," Mike says.

Ted glances at me. "Okay."

"Not well, is how it went."

"Did she tell you she's engaged?" I ask.

"I don't want to talk about it."

We stare out the window, listening to the sound of Ted's chewing. It is that time of night when nothing makes anything better, a time of lingering over what could have been. The number of birthday candles grows, the internships mount, parents keep nagging; there is no more energy to wind up the dream. The song stops. It's just three blind mice with nowhere to go on a Friday night.

And in that enduring silence, it occurs to me where we can go.

"You were right," says Mike. "This is nice."

The three of us stand over the vent with our hands out, like it's a bonfire. The wafts of steam toast our bones.

"You just can't leave," says Ted. "The longer you stay, the colder it'll be to leave."

"I don't care," says Mike. "I like this."

So we stay awhile, letting time go by.

"Do you remember your great-great-great-grandparents?" I ask.

"Nope."

"Not one bit." Mike shakes his head.

"Yeah," I say. "Neither do I. But we're all typecast to be forgotten great-great-great-grandparents, aren't we?"

"Here's my hot take: I don't think we die," says Ted. "I think life breaks up with you."

The steam soaks into my socks. I am wet, the air is cold, but the vent keeps me warm. I see across the street that Casablanca, a restaurant based on the movie, has closed. It was the first movie I saw with Soph, *Casablanca*. That mattered once. But part of the "friends" job description is to remember that the whole thing lasted a month, and people come and go, and in the panorama view, life is as long as it is short.

"She friend-zoned me," Mike says out of nowhere. "She said we could hang out as buds."

"Nice." Ted winces.

"I mean, what do you even say to that?" Mike asks.

I whisper to myself, and then say aloud, "I think this is the beginning of a beautiful friendship."

the last
american pie
(november)

My Thanksgiving holiday plans are set to be an idyllic sequel of last year. Last Thanksgiving, I was invited by an old-money friend named Fisher Roach to his girlfriend's parent's vacation house in Nantucket. Her family goes there during the November offseason. I went, thinking it was the best of two bad options: fly back home for a midwestern nag-fest of uncles and aunts or stay in Massachusetts with rich strangers. I chose the strangers, and as it turned out, it was the opposite of a better bad choice. It was a weekend with the children of America's extravagant where money became a frivolous burden. I stayed in the "kids' house," a beachside mansion with eleven other college kids, all beautiful, many expecting upward of $30 to $60 million upon their parents' deaths.

One girl took a liking to me, and I didn't stop her. Beyond

that eerie beauty of the rich, she had exquisite taste in movies. We watched *Jules and Jim* in the projector room after all had gone to bed, and then slept there and in the morning acted like it never happened. After a day of the "kids" exploring Nantucket in new Jeeps, hopping in and out of restaurants for nibbles of Oysters Rockefeller and white wine, I attended Thanksgiving dinner at the main family house. A moderate, stoic staff worked that Thanksgiving weekend. I in no way belonged there with my fake cashmere sweater, and yet there I was, making drunk, bored wives laugh. It took me three hours to recognize a Botox laugh. I was known as "Fisher's little writer friend." The rich enjoy having artists around them, and the children of the rich have this perverse obsession to be accepted by the poor. With my glasses and with Fisher mentioning I once helped him write an essay, I became the "writer friend." I was hooked. The rich life suited me. I spread caviar on my toast the first morning there. Juice was always freshly squeezed. Any sort of normal life after this would hurt. Fisher's girlfriend, Mia, was suspicious of me until she saw how much I made her mother laugh. Mia stands five-foot-five in heels and is full of romantic ideals that will not settle for anything less than what she saw in 90s rom-coms. Fisher, whom she met in DC where they clerked for rival senators, is a sophisticated character with the graceful manners of an old man. They became some strange ideal for me since that weekend. Their faces symmetrical, their hair never out of place. I can easily see them marrying and having pretty babies in Cape Cod.

The rich liked me, and I liked being liked by them. They could afford to like me. Their money erased the big life problems and in the absence of those kinds of problems, they could afford to be kind. I lived the business class life without ever buying a ticket.

A few weeks ago, Fisher said I was invited back, if I don't have any other Thanksgiving plans, that is. It seems I was a big hit.

It got gray in Boston and the faces of strangers hardened. To the distress of the fashion-conscious it was time for the parkas. Boston weather is like this: it teases you in October with the occasional freak snowstorm, returns to sweater weather, and then one mid-November morning it becomes Canada. A climate in perpetual identity crisis.

At 10:14 p.m., I sit in an enclave of DVDs in the Lamont Library basement floor. I'm procrastinating with a documentary on the development of the Helvetica font which is somehow more interesting than Intro to Psych 102. Ten p.m. is the lonely hour. It is the end of the day, close to any rational form of bedtime, and yet here we are at the library, reaching for nothing.

I pause the documentary and walk upstairs to the library café for more terrible coffee. I smile at someone who I think smiles at me, but she looks away, talking to someone through her AirPods. Sitting three tables away from her, I see Fisher and Mia. They're in a tight table for two, facing each other as if playing chess. They're arguing. Fisher's eyes land on me for a millisecond but he doesn't register me. Or maybe he does and pretends not to. They argue in that subdued sort of way that looks civil and feels subtle but is still so obviously not. A muted, ugly fight.

I order a black coffee which appears to annoy the barista; to brew a whole pot for the cheapest thing on the menu. As I wait, I glance over at Fisher and Mia's table. A few whispered words slip through.

"Lunch . . . not what I'm saying . . . no, stop . . ."

The coffee machine is an old one that brews in a loud gargle as if little factory workers are inside it. It fills the room with another source of noise to muffle Fisher and Mia's arguing. Gargle. "Stop saying that." Gargle. "You're gaslighting." Gargle. "Are you hearing yourself?" Gargle. After an awkward pause, Mia jolts up from her chair. Different heads glance their direction.

In a penetrating alto, she yells, "IT'S NOT ABOUT THE MUFFIN!"

It's a scream that echoes in the same volume as a cry

for help. All movement in the room stops. Everyone is looking, wondering. She storms out an emergency exit but the alarm does not go off. There aren't even the whispers among strangers that usually follow an outburst like this. Only stares. Fisher rolls his eyes, stretches his neck, and stands up and calmly follows her out the emergency exit into the cold.

The noise of the coffee machine fades into a hissing cough of steam. After a few puffs, my cheap black coffee is ready.

"It's not about the muffin?" Nora asks.

"Yep."

"What does it mean, what muffin?"

"I don't know."

"Were they eating a muffin?"

"No."

At 3:18 p.m. I meet Nora, Mike, and Ted for a debriefing lunch.

"Maybe they were arguing about the difference between a cupcake and a muffin," Mike suggests.

"What, the ongoing muffin-cupcake debate? That's what does it?" I say, "I haven't been able to think about anything else. It's like some mental curse. What could they have possibly been arguing about?"

"How loud was she?" Ted asks.

"The loudest I've ever heard a human being be."

"I like a loud woman. It's a turn-on." He studies the lunch menu as if we haven't been here dozens of times.

"Maybe she wanted a muffin, and he didn't get the hint," Nora suggests.

"Then what? What led to her exploding like that?"

"I don't know. Why does it matter?"

"You realize, if they break up, my Thanksgiving plans are doomed," I say.

"Why?" Nora asks.

"I'm Fisher's friend. It's Mia's family's house. If they break up, Mia isn't going to invite just me."

"That's true," Mike confirms. "That's friendship poaching, a strict violation of the breakup rules of engagement."

"Just go home for Thanksgiving like a normal person," Ted suggests.

"Have you seen flight prices going home now? They're in the eight-hundreds." Not to mention I don't have the money to go back home even if I chose to.

A bored waitress with a nose ring comes to take Ted's order. "Are you ready now?"

"Yes," Ted clears his throat. "I'll get the chicken sandwich, but can you switch out the chicken for roast beef, and instead of lettuce, I want Swiss cheese."

"So, that would be a roast beef sandwich . . . ," she says.

"No, I just want a chicken sandwich with a few changes."

"Right, but if you adjust it too much, it becomes a different sandwich."

"I'm a little confused," Ted brings out his negotiating smirk. "How many changes does it take for a thing to become a different thing?"

"Chicken to roast beef. That's a big change."

"How about this: just give me a plate of roast beef with a side of toast, but don't toast the toast," he says.

"I'm just going to put your order down as a roast beef sandwich."

"No, don't."

"Why not?"

"Because it costs more."

On a Tuesday, Mike calls to tell me our jazz band is playing the national anthem at the Harvard vs. Yale hockey game. By the time I realize he's being serious, I feel nauseated. This will be an audience of three thousand people.

The soprano scheduled months ago to sing the anthem canceled due to strep throat. Plan B was a country singer, who canceled upon finding out he'd be on the upcoming season of *The Bachelorette*. There was no Plan C and it was four days before the game.

The head of PR for the Harvard hockey club heard Louis

Armstrong's version of the anthem and sold himself on this delusion that we could do the same thing. Mike didn't correct him. The PR guy could have picked one of the many registered jazz clubs on campus, but Mike cozied up to him through poker night, and evidently one of these nights led to this gig.

We start panic practicing that night. Executive order. As we're setting up our instruments in one of the music rooms in Memorial Hall, Ted has an announcement: "I don't want to do the national anthem."

Mike and I exchange glances, waiting for him to say he's joking.

"It's corny," he adds.

"It's tradition," says Mike. "There are songs you mess with, and there are songs you don't. The national anthem is a song you don't."

"Then they shouldn't have picked a jazz band," Ted ruffles his hair. "I mean c'mon. Do you not feel like mainstream sellouts?"

"This will be our biggest audience, Ted. Let's not blow it," I say.

"We're already blowing it by not trying something special," he grumbles. "There is no way—zero chance—that Miles Davis would've just played the national anthem."

"We're not Miles Davis."

"We're not even jazz musicians with this BS." He throws an empty water bottle at the trash can and misses.

The next morning I check airline prices again. Even ones with a 4:30 a.m. departure have breached the thousand-dollar mark. It's been a few days since their fight; they've surely resolved things by now. I call Fisher up to check, just in case.

"Hello?" he answers.

"Hey, Fisher, it's Charlie."

"Oh, hey, Charlie."

"Say, are you and Mia going to the hockey game tomorrow?"

"Yeah."

"How are you guys?"

I shouldn't have asked so quickly. He pauses one second too long. Maybe he did see me in the library that night. "Things are good, things are good. You know, finals."

"Same, same. I'm looking forward to Thanksgiving again. I used to hate it because I never felt thankful for turkey. But wow, last year was, wow . . ."

Silence.

"So," I say, "I wanted to ask, are we driving up together like last time?"

"Um . . ." he hesitates. "Yeah. Sure. We'll see what happens."

"Okay. Let me know," I say. "Do you guys want to do something before the game?"

"Um. Sure, we can."

"Let's do it. I'll walk with you and Mia from the Quad, do a proper pregame thing."

"We can do that."

"Looking forward to it. How's Mia?" I ask.

"She's good," he stops there.

"You guys all good? Any issues?" I go in for the kill. "I ask because you're just sounding a little off right now."

"No, all's good. I just have a lot on."

This time, I pause. He doesn't seem bothered by it.

"Okay, so I'll see you tomorrow?" I ask.

"Sounds good."

"See you tomorrow," I say.

"Yep."

He hangs up. The situation is worse than I thought.

I learn that melatonin gummies do not mute a preoccupied brain. The clock reads 3:03 a.m. *It's not about the muffin.* I say it aloud in bed staring at the ceiling. Maybe the muffin is code for something. Maybe it refers to a body part. A standard blueberry muffin has an average of thirty-seven grams of sugar. A cupcake has an average of thirty-six grams of sugar. One is eaten for breakfast; one is eaten at birthday parties. If you were to bring muffins to a birthday party, people would think you weren't fun. Bring a cupcake to breakfast, and people would think you were out of control. We agree to stand in line, to shake hands, that money is valuable, that a muffin is for breakfast and that a cupcake is not.

I walk to the Radcliffe Quadrangle ("the Quad") with my sax case by my side and a book called *How to Turn Your Life Around*. I've read half of it and still have no idea how to even turn my underwear around.

My body is tense with anxiety from multiple fronts. The thought of having no money, of Fisher and Mia calling it quits and screwing up my holiday plans, of rising flight prices, of my now faltering grades because of my mental preoccupation with this muffin thing. What a mess. I could quickly join a cult in such a vulnerable state.

Fisher and Mia are housed at Cabot and Pfoho. I wander the east wing of Pfoho House, passing beige IKEA tables and café lamps placed over sofas from a different decade. The place is modern compared to the rest of the Harvard dormitories. It looks unfinished, as if abandoned after once being a discount furniture shop.

Fisher messages that they'll be down shortly. I sit on a worn-out sofa near the elevators. A mouse runs by. I shut my eyes for a moment and think to the ceiling. Not praying, but almost praying. Maybe that my only shot at happiness this year not go up in flames.

Fisher and Mia come out of the elevator, formally dressed. She wears a thin satin maxi with a suggestive slit at her leg, but her efforts are covered with a puffer jacket. In that very second, everything seems resolved. I sense no tension.

"Sorry we're late," Mia says to me with a serious look. "I couldn't find my eyeliner."

"I told you, you look fine without it," Fisher insists.

"I look horrible without it. Why are you always saying that? Do you want me to look bad?"

"Why would I want you to look bad?"

She turns to me. "Can we take the shuttle?"

My last milligram of hope that prayer or the power of positive thinking works, is gone. We ride the shuttle to the Square and then cross Weeks Bridge with scarce, unmemorable conversation.

I've been to the Bright-Landry Hockey Center four times and every time it smells like cheap soap and mildew. It looks as if it hasn't changed since 1993, but it's strangely better that way, the way most memorable moments involve defect.

About eight hundred Yale fans make a showing but it's mostly a sea of crimson in the crowd. The players warm up when we arrive, making mad circles and popping pucks at their goalies. Buddy Holly's "Peggy Sue" plays through the loudspeakers.

Fisher and Mia buy their tickets from a man with a

striking resemblance to Lyndon B. Johnson. Scarf-wearing fans, beanies, beer, nachos, and hot chocolates steam past. We find our seats above the penalty box. It's ten minutes before I need to practice "The Star-Spangled Banner" in one of the locker rooms. I hum it in my head, trying to remind myself how it goes.

"Are you cold?" Fisher asks Mia.

"No," she lies, covering her arms.

"Are you sure?"

"I'm fine, leave me alone. God."

Suddenly a half-dozen sweaters embroidered with "Yale University" flank us in the bleachers. They all seem to know Fisher as he gives them routine handshakes and half hugs. This one girl possessing a toned glutei maximi greets Fisher with a hug that lasts a second too long. Mia delivers a subtle, private glare to the owner of these toned glutei maximi.

"So glad you all could make it," Fisher croons, a real Mr. Nice Guy all of a sudden.

"You think we'd miss seeing Harvard lose one?" The girl has a fantastically breathy voice, like she thinks everything she says is charming. "Also, what's the plan after? Are we all doing dinner?"

"Yes." Fisher glances at Mia.

"I can't wait. We haven't spoken in so long. Not in person at least."

The napkin Mia holds becomes twisted mulch. A certain kind of angst washes over me, like when I first learned the family dog wouldn't live forever. Fisher and the girl possessing the toned glutei maximi are suddenly off in their own world entranced in some conversation. I sit with Mia and feel helpless.

"How've you been, Charlie?" Mia turns to me, seeking distraction.

"How've I been? Mia," I say. "It's okay. I know you and Fisher are going through it. You don't have to tell me if you don't want to, but if you need an ear, you can use me."

Her eyes look away for a moment and then come back to me. "Has he said anything?"

"No."

She shakes her head, staring into the distance. "I don't think we're going to make it, Charlie. Everyone can see it. It's not just that the honeymoon stage is over. It's the whole story." She swallows. If she's fighting tears, she's doing it well.

"You know when I knew?" she asks me. "When I knew we fell out of love? About a week ago, we went to karaoke downtown with some friends, and "American Pie" came on. You know the song "American Pie"? That's our song. It played on our first date and we bonded over the fact that we knew every word until the fourth verse." She laughs at this thought. "That song is the one thing that makes him glance at me the

way he did. We sang "American Pie" and it felt like nothing
was ever wrong. Anyway . . ."

Her words drift off and she stares at the hockey players
practicing, suddenly ignoring me. I sit there for about two
minutes not knowing what else to do. Then I decide to go.

"I'm going," I tell Fisher, gesturing at my sax. "I have to
practice."

"We'll see you after, for dinner?" He turns to me
half-heartedly, like I'm disturbing him.

I tell him yes, whatever, and leave. I have to get away
from this Greek tragedy, as far and as quickly away as possible. I feel like I've grown up seven years since sitting down.

The deep burps of Mike's double bass and Ted's guitar echo
in some vacant locker room downstairs as they practice "The
Star-Spangled Banner." Nora is here too, hoping to meet a cute
hockey player. The "hockey smell" of sweat and rubber is an
unforgettable scent. It reeks the halls with boughs of mildew.

No one greets me when I enter, which is somehow touching. I remember the first time I realized I had a good friend,
when Mike told me I looked terrible one day.

"You ever look at some people, and they just look like
they'd have bad breath?" Ted leafs through the roster of the
hockey team.

"Ted, do you even think about the things you think

about?" Nora earnestly inquires this like she's trying to finally understand him.

"Do you ever think about the things you don't think about?" Ted shoots back.

I sit down, thinking of Mia and Fisher, whistling "American Pie."

"See, that's what we should play." Ted points at me. "Not this Star-Spangled Bullshit."

"Ted, we talked about this," says Mike.

"Remember when we had to play American Pie at that bar mitzvah?" Ted says. "We even know it."

I start assembling my sax and whisper about what's wrong with the world. I guess Nora hears me. "What happened with you?"

"Who died?" Mike asks. "Is it Henry Kissinger, yes or no?"

"No one's dead," I say. "You know Fisher and Mia?"

"No," says Nora.

"Remember the 'it's not about the muffin' couple?"

"Oh, I remember."

"They're calling it quits. My Thanksgiving plans are sunk. No Nantucket, no nothing."

"Well, there goes your dream of marrying rich," Mike says.

Ted starts humming a mouth-trumpet rendition of "American Pie."

"Also," I add. "It's also just sad. They were a great couple. They were like the epitome of a good relationship. I mean, Jesus, if they don't make it, who will?"

"You put your idea of a good relationship on a random college fling?" Nora clarifies.

"All right, go to hell. It's crazy, I know."

"What about all the princess movies?" Nora says. "They're worse. I was in a bad relationship for months because I thought I was Belle and he was the Beast. I thought if I was just patient and kind enough, he would transform. It didn't happen. He was still a beast. End of story."

"Sue Disney then."

"What if they announce, 'Ladies and gentlemen, please stand for our national anthem,' and instead of the anthem, we play 'American Pie,'" Ted says. He snickers like this is the funniest thing he's heard.

"No, we should play 'Hawaii Five-O.'" Mike thinks his joke is better and starts playing the theme to Hawaii Five-O on his bass.

And then, the idea occurs to me. "But what if we actually did?" I say this to myself and then to them. "What if we just played 'American Pie'?"

"Instead of the anthem?"

"Why not? I mean, it's the most beloved American song; it tells the story of America—it does everything the national anthem does." I only realize this conclusion as I'm suggesting it.

"Hey, what's with you guys? What's so hard about just doing the national anthem?" Mike asks.

"I'm dead serious about this." I look them right in the eye so they know I'm not messing around.

"Yeah, see," Ted chimes in. "This is what I'm talking about."

"Wouldn't people get mad?" Nora asks.

"Why would they? These academic yuppies, they have no sense of patriotism," I tell them. "And Mike, if we really wanted attention, this will do it. The *Harvard Crimson* will write about this for the next three days. We'll go viral. We might make national news. I'm telling you: the crowd will love it."

I can tell Mike is thinking about it. He has that look in his eye. People go quiet when they're really considering something.

Ted is already on board. "'American Pie' is basically a second national anthem."

"It'd be like comic relief," Mike mumbles to himself. "Everyone's expecting the anthem, and wham—'A long, long, time ago' . . ."

"Exactly."

"No," says Nora. "You're going to get in trouble."

"I say we do it."

"Yeah, me too." Ted stands firm.

"Guys, no," Nora's voice gets serious.

"Mike?"

Mike bites his nail, pacing the floor. He looks at me. I look at him. He looks at Ted. Ted looks at him. He looks at Nora. Nora looks at me.

"All right," he says. "Let's do it. Let's stick it to the man." In a minute he'll act like this was his idea.

We practice the song until the third verse. After that, I don't know, the song gets too long or something. Ted and Mike experiment with the verse's bass and guitar parts. I'll be leading with the sax. We know most of it from the last bar mitzvah gig we played. Nora doesn't think our plan is too hot. Ted tells her she's oppressing our full creative potential with her toxic femininity.

Someone knocks on the door, a metallic, clunky knock. A referee with a handlebar mustache tells us we're on soon. Nora wishes us good luck and babbles something in French, shaking her head.

The players return to the locker room from their warm-ups. Two Zambonis roll onto the ice and smooth it up like window wipers. They finish and groan off. The lights go down, and melodramatic music plays under introductions of the three captains from each team. The announcer sounds like he's from the 1930s. You can tell he loves the sound of his own voice. He announces each player in that weird way: "Mark . . . Ferrrrlingggg!" The Harvard fans boo the Yale players, and the Yale fans boo the Harvard players.

This is our cue. I step onto the ice first, Mike and Ted following. I nearly break my neck walking on the fresh ice. Ice is fine to walk on, but when it's fresh, it's slick. The light show stops flickering and displays misty shades of red, white, and blue on the ice. The three captains from each team line up on the blue line, helmets off, bowing their heads like it's the rapture or something. I smell that "hockey smell" on their jerseys.

We get up to the three microphones at center ice, adjusting the angles to our lips.

"And now, ladies and gentlemen . . ." The announcer puts on this phony somber voice to really sell it. "Please rise for the presentation of our national anthem."

The sound of two thousand butts rising from bleachers is like a war drum. It's funny how you can't get ten people in one room to shut up, and yet when a baritone announcer asks two thousand people to put a cork in it, they obey. The silence of an arena is different. Everything echoes.

It suddenly occurs to me what a bad idea this is. For chrissake, what are we thinking?

But then I think of Nantucket. Of the caviar on toast in the morning. The jeeps tearing up the sand. The girl I saw

Jules et Jim with. Then I think, maybe the craziest thing you can do with your life is to not do the crazy thing.

I lean down to speak into the microphone meant for my sax. "We'd like to dedicate this to Fisher and Mia."

Mike and Ted look at me with utter confusion. An echoey silence faces us.

Mike arranges his fingers on the bass. Ted readies the first chord. My lips kiss the mouthpiece.

I begin to solo on the sax with the opening parts.

When performing in front of judgmental eyes, time becomes slow or very fast. All I can think of in this moment is how long four-and-a-half billion years old is and how long this floating rock has been spinning, which is to say a long, long time, and here I am wondering what's for breakfast the morning after Thanksgiving in Nantucket. I can't decide if that's sad or not. So, I keep playing, my eyes shut tight, trying to enjoy the passage of time.

The crowd starts to sing along. I can't believe it. "Bye, bye, Miss American pie." They clap their hands to the chorus with even a little sway in their hips. It's a movie moment. We have them rolling with an unstoppable momentum. Mike never played better bass in his life. The deep sound of it plays perfectly against the chorus of the crowd. The arena bellows with the communal voices of rivals, putting aside their troubles, coming together, joined in pride and music, to sing their hearts out for something greater than themselves.

This is not what happens.

The booing begins with one wise guy. That's all it takes. Some beer voice with no inflection. Whoever the hell he is, he sounds like his name is Chaz. A higher-pitched "boo" joins him, probably his girlfriend Jessica or something. Chaz and Jess, perfect. There's always that one high-pitched "boo" above the monotone that gets everyone else going. Everyone joins them, and I mean everyone. And these aren't just any kind of "boos," they're aggressive "boos." I can feel the sound waves hitting us from all angles. Mike keeps playing. He doesn't know what to do, and neither do I.

We only get to the second verse, rushing through to the chorus to the point where it almost sounds like experimental jazz. Do we even bother to finish? We can no longer hear ourselves play. The booing has taken over and our microphones are turned off. As we're walking off the ice—tiny, careful steps, like we're ninety years old—the booing doesn't stop. It never does.

We sneak out an emergency exit near the locker rooms. A hockey crowd is like no other. In a sport where the athletes remove gloves and punch each other's faces, I'm not taking chances with the fans. We pack up our instruments, arguing about what went wrong.

Eventually I can't take it. Mike thinks we shouldn't have done it, Ted thinks we should have sung it, and I'm tired of listening. I step outside the locker room to move my legs around. A prerecorded public domain version of the national anthem is playing.

The game begins. The flow of people and noise snakes through the arena when I try to find Nora. As I weave through crowds of Yale blue and Harvard crimson, some no doubt future CEOs, I spot Mia. Her expression blooms with a deep, uninhibited smile that I've never seen before. I think a man remembers vividly all the times he's made a woman happy. This will be one of those days; a dangerous one, in a way. The feeling of making someone feel this good is an addiction that can override your whole life just to keep supplying that joy. For now, those wisdoms are out the window. I've made someone smile, and that's that.

"Charlie, what the hell," she says with that excellent smile of hers. "You're crazy. That was absolutely insane."

"Did you like it?" I ask.

"Did I like it? Oh my God, that was everything."

Fisher spots me through a sea of bobbling heads and pats a few shoulders so he can come to say something. "Man, Charlie," he is shocked and happy, like a man who found his purpose. "That was the most baller move I've ever seen. Did you tell him to do that?" He looks at Mia.

"I thought you made him do it!" Mia laughs, touching his hand. "My heart stopped when you said our names."

"Everyone was booing," he tells me. "We were the only ones singing along—"

"And everyone looked at us like we were terrorists," she adds.

"It was nuts! We were so excited we started dancing when the chorus came and then people started booing *us*."

"Oh God, that was the crazy part," she says. "It was like being hated by the world for ten seconds. But it was exhilarating too; we were the only ones singing along."

"Charlie, buddy, are you okay?" He grips my shoulder. "I can't even imagine what it was like being down there."

"I love you guys." I say straight to their faces, "I love you guys, really."

Mia holds my arm. "Charlie, that was a beautiful and very stupid thing you did down there."

She looks at Fisher who looks back at her with the same relaxed affection. They each hug me. I have this sudden urge to cry out of relief. Despite all that's wrong with life, you can still hold small flashes of joy that fight the dark like fireworks in the night. No matter how completely you foul up your life, somehow these flashes keep you going on the promise you can start over. You can begin again, I think in that moment. You can begin again.

Fisher shakes my hand and gives me another side hug and says he'll contact me about driving up to Nantucket soon.

As I watch them leave, I remember something. Something vital. A part of me says, "Don't. Just leave it be." But I can't. I run up to them.

"Hey, Fisher, Mia." They turn around. "Hey, look, sorry, this is going to sound weird, but I've got to ask. It's kind of funny actually." I fake a laugh to make it look like it's a light, nothing question. "A few days ago, you guys were at the Lamont Library Café, remember? It was late, you were talking, I was ordering coffee, and at one point, Mia, you yell 'it's not about the muffin.' That has been bugging me for days. What was all that about?"

Mia's eyes look down with a minor grin. Fisher's eyes look up with a minor grin. "Oh, that was nothing," he assures me.

"Yeah, but why the muffin? What's not about the muffin?" I ask.

He strokes his eyebrow with a thumb. "Nothing. I don't really remember to be honest."

"Look, this has been eating at me. I've been coming up with theories on what you meant. What could you have possibly been arguing about?"

Mia scratches the back of her ear. "Well, I'll let Fisher explain that."

He takes one step away from her, looking on with disgust. "You want me to explain? I find it adorable that you think the burden is on me to explain."

"If you can't take responsibility, I don't know what to tell you."

"You can start with sorry," he says.

She rolls her eyes with a look of resignation. "Never mind."

"Never mind what?"

She doesn't respond. She crosses her arms and walks away.

"Okay then," Fisher turns to me. "I'll keep you posted about what's happening for the weekend."

"Wait, Fisher, please, what was the muffin thing about?" I beg for his answer.

He acts like he doesn't hear me as he turns away.

We don't stay for the game. Nora takes me, Mike, and Ted to Le's, the Vietnamese restaurant, for dinner, thinking warm pho is the beginning to any healing journey. She's being hyperbolic, but she's not entirely wrong.

"I'm done, I quit, I'm never playing again," I swear. "We're finished, you know. Everyone knows our faces. We're screwed."

"You're not going to quit," Nora says. "You guys had nothing to lose before, and you have nothing to lose now. You were nobodies before tonight, and you'll be nobodies after tonight."

"Thank you, that makes everything better."

"How were we, though, on a scale of one to ten?" Ted asks.

She slurps her oolong tea. "Bad."

"How bad?"

"Season eight, *Game of Thrones* bad."

"That's it, I'm done," I announce. "I'm going to overdose on probiotics tonight."

Nora sighs. "After tonight, your luck is so bad, there's no place to go but up."

She's right. I can't die. The new Dunkin' Donuts fall flavors haven't come out yet. And besides, if I die, what was it all for? I used to think it was love. The way I see it now, life is like being invited to a mostly lame party where the main selling point is a limited supply of delicious lemon bars. I like lemon bars, but is that really a reason to endure the party?

In some twisted coincidence, Fisher and Mia walk into the damn restaurant. They're seated at a middle table with about twelve of their Yale and Harvard friends. The restaurant is suddenly crowded. They each have a subtle air of entitlement that dominates the space. They break chopsticks and look at menus and do whatever you do at restaurants. Fisher sits next to the blond Yale woman with that breathy-as-hell voice. Mia keeps shifting her weight and drinking her water too often. Fisher makes the girl laugh. Our music didn't save anyone.

Nora pays for our meal, in honor of our rough night. As we stand up to leave, I pass by Fisher and Mia's table. Neither of them stops me as I walk by. For a millisecond maybe, I think Fisher notices me, but his focus belongs to someone new. As I step out the door, I look back one last time to see if they look up, but they are already beyond me.

I would like to think of them as they were, a Camelot you could never quite reach. Perhaps that perfection only ever existed in my head. But wherever it lived, I decide then to press Pause, turn off the perfect story while it's still perfect in my head, and stop watching before it ends.

On the way out, passing a Chinese takeout stand, Nora grabs a handful of fortune cookies from a "thank you" box. She gives us each a fortune as we walk down Mt. Auburn St.

Mike reads his: "Embrace winds of change for they will lead you to new frontiers."

Ted: "Mine just says, 'Face facts with dignity.'"

Nora squints at hers under the streetlight: "Mine says, 'You either swim or sink like a stone.'" She turns to me, seeing I haven't opened mine. "What's yours?"

"I don't want to open it."

"You should always open fortune cookies. There's always a chance it tells you what life's all about."

"I already know what life's all about."

"What is it, then?"

"I don't know, but it's sure not about the muffin."

what's up, god?

(december)

I was once a very religious person, and sometimes I miss being that person, or at least everything related to being that person. I am constantly chasing that feeling of finishing a good novel, because it's that same feeling you get in church on Sunday, getting directions to heaven. Reading a novel never feels like writing one, just as giving advice never feels like taking it. Reading is easier than writing, but giving advice is easier than taking it.

It is 10:21 a.m. on a Sunday in December. Temperature, 35 degrees. Nora and I walk to a church without coffee, exchanging secrets of the opposite sex. She swears the inner wrists are an overlooked part of a woman's senses, and then the conversation quickly turns to eggs.

"An egg is an egg." She stretches her neck into some half-hearted yoga position.

"But how you prepare an egg makes it a different food. Scrambled eggs are so unlike boiled eggs, they shouldn't even be considered the same."

"That is like saying every religion is the same as long as they're trying to get to God."

"Well, they are, sort of."

"But how can you say that? You'd disregard every religion as the same?"

"Religion, politics, eggs—they are just different ways of getting to the same place."

Nora sneezes and then accuses me of agnosticism.

"I'm not agnostic," I say in my defense.

"You're not *not* agnostic."

"Look, I think there's something called God, I just don't think we have the whole story," I explain. "And besides, life after death makes for a great retirement plan."

Nora's Quebecois identity is inescapably tied to her Catholicism, so convincing her to sit through a Protestant service for free food was not easy. After I told her how much money I was saving from the free meals with the Methodists, she reconsidered her religion.

Nora recently had a falling out with her family over how to divert their charity budget: Lyme disease research or the Clothe Nora Foundation. As a show of protest, she vowed not to use their credit cards. She lasted about ninety minutes before calling me up for advice on how to live in poverty with dignity—in which I am an expert.

"How did you meet this guy?" Nora asks, referring to the guy that first brought me to church.

Here's what happened. Last month I was eating breakfast with Ted in the Adams House dining hall, going on about watery scrambled eggs. I was in a bad mood. This guy wearing a Newt Gingrich 2008 T-shirt overheard us, came over, introduced himself as Maugham, and invited us both to Sunday service on the premise of "non-watery eggs" for brunch. Like ideological jujitsu, he knew where my pressure points were. I'd seen him on campus, always alone, shy-looking, wearing strange clothes like Newt Gingrich shirts.

Ted didn't go, since he planned on fornicating with a gentile that Sunday, but I combed my hair, stole a Bible, and went. I was hungry and low on money. Even one free meal this week would help to patch the rapidly sinking ship known as the SS *Savings Account*.

The service was about thanking God for unanswered prayers or something. I can't remember. The hunger had reached my ears by that point. It was a pitiful hunger, the kind that reminds you you're poor. All I know is that the bald pastor is divorced. He managed to mention it about four times in one sermon.

Then the food was finally served in the dining hall.

Rosemary quiche. When this buttery goodness entered me, every suppressed memory activated, like reliving childhood.

Maugham was excited to see me, or at least he pretended well. What a strange guy. It's like he transitioned wrong from that awkward stage at fifteen and never quite left it. He's the over-parented type, where university is such a new environment, it changes you like boot camp.

As a thank-you, I gave him this gym membership card I had. I had originally gotten it from Mike, who gave it to me because he broke up with a CrossFit girl he was dating.

"Oh, thank you," Maugham said. "I don't really work out, but thank you."

"I was wondering . . ." I looked around. "Could I take some of these leftovers home?"

"Well . . ." He looked unsure.

"And I forgot," I jumped in. "This gym membership is good for seven months, so enjoy."

If there's anything we've learned from mothers, it is the art of guilt-tripping. Maugham caved and even got me Tupperware.

After a month of free meals, I brought Nora into this operation.

We arrive as the bell rings. I can tell Nora is lightly impressed by the idyllic presentation. It must remind her of home, whatever that means to her.

I see Maugham wearing that dental-commercial smile of his, but he is not dressed in his usual Sunday suit. He's replaced it with white sneakers and a yellow tracksuit. I guess he downgraded from business casual to *Kill Bill*.

"Charlie, I never truly thanked you for that gym membership," Maugham says.

"How's that going for you?"

"Incredible, actually. Like, unbelievable. I've been going every day," he says. "I'm doing a five-K this week. I feel like a new man. I never played sports as a kid. My dad was an overbearing father, you know . . ."

He rambles about his upbringing, but it all merges into a forgettable cluster.

The service this fine morning is about the book of Job, and I actually listen this time. Nora gets right into it with the singing and shaking of hands with strangers. She knows only the traditional church songs. She is stunned by the lack of Holy Communion or kneeling for a Hail Mary.

Then it is time to eat.

The smell of the rosemary quiche tingles my arm hairs. We don't have many gentle December afternoons left in Boston. Dining in suits feels like a wedding. The fireplace in the dining hall is dutifully fed by a little boy in overalls. The youth pastor leads us in another prayer in thanks for modern medicine, rent-controlled housing, and free parking.

I show Nora how to sneak food into Tupperware. First, you overload your plate with two or three meals at the buffet, and then you carefully slide chunks from your plate onto your lap, where the Tupperware catches them. I have this all figured out.

Nora tries the quiche. "Oh my God."

"Right?"

"Oh my God, it is fantastic."

"I'm telling you, it's the best quiche in town."

"Do not talk," she says. "I want to enjoy this completely."

As I sip coffee, Maugham strides over and sits at our table. He has no plate, only a protein shake. Nora is peeved at his presence and probably "disrespectful" Sunday attire.

Maugham explains why he has no plate, and this explanation inevitably turns to health advice. I know Nora cannot eat with a rambler. It's funny what people can and cannot eat with. Mike can't eat with a loud chewer, and I can't eat with someone who watches me eat like they're going to write about it later.

"Do you think Jesus exercised?" Nora asks, changing the subject. She can't stand people giving health advice. Oddly enough, she gives it all the time, but people are the worst violators of their own pet peeves.

"Are you asking if Jesus was healthy?" Maugham asks.

"No, I mean did Jesus exercise, like cardio?"

"Jogging wasn't common practice until the 1980s."

"But did Jesus know exercise was good for the body? He gave us all this advice on how to live but nothing about living long. Suspicious, no?"

I forgot to warn her not to bring this stuff up in a church. The trick is to stay a little complicated with your beliefs, and they tend to leave you alone.

"It's plausible that men would lift heavy objects and gain muscle from that," Maugham says.

"I suppose if God could lift, it would be pointless." She takes a sizable bite of quiche and by her orgasmic expression, savors every teaspoon of butter.

Maugham clears his throat. "Why do you say that?"

"He is God. If he cannot lift more than anybody on earth, who is he then? As that old saying goes, if God can make a stone he cannot lift, is he still God?"

By the blank look on Maugham's face, this question is clearly new to him.

"So who is he, if he is not God?" he asks.

"I don't know."

"Identity theft is not a joke," I say to cut the tension.

Nora sips her Americano, satisfied that her line of reasoning makes Maugham go away with a pondering tightness in his lips. I don't think he fully buys her logic, but perhaps he doesn't understand it.

I don't care at this point. I am happy with my quiche and the thought of being free of finals in a month. I've always found something happy about a church. It reminds me of being a kid, somehow, a time I could feel ambivalent about failure.

The week goes by uneventfully, except for the things that happen. We study for finals. I forget what I am studying. Nora thinks this is a joke, but I'm absolutely serious. All I know is I'm writing a paper called, "Joseph Goebbels and the Latency Period."

Mike and I watch a hockey game against Dartmouth and then get a burger at Grafton Street. He orders a milkshake and lays out his emotional laundry.

"I enrolled in a Brazilian jujitsu class," he says. "I'm told I have the body for it."

"What kind of body is that?"

"Good calf muscles. The instructor thought they were implants."

"Are you still in the chess club?"

"They said I'm too emotional for it. I kept protecting the queen and forfeiting the king because I'm subconsciously submissive toward overbearing mother figures."

"And a fight club was the next alternative?"

"I mean, it's like chess, but with your body."

"But you aren't good at chess."

A psychic once said Mike's handwriting is so cramped and dense because he longs for closer connections to people. I've always suspected his key motive was to belong to something.

"Nora and I are going to the church tomorrow," I tell him. "You should come, you know? Free food, you might meet someone."

"Nah, I don't buy that stuff."

"All you have to do is sit through a sermon about not masturbating or something, and then you get free food that lasts two days," I tell him.

"I have fight club on Sunday."

The next week Nora and I waltz into church at 10:59. The emcee offers no expression and does not give us a pamphlet. It is an awkward moment, and with my hand stretched out while walking past him, I high-five his elbow. Nora tells me something is off.

"Nothing's off," I insist.

"Then what was that?" Her chin points behind us. People are glancing our way. We find our seats in the back, which provides cover for our backpacks full of empty Tupperware.

The service is about "not fearing to spread the gospel." The pastor asks the congregation to follow along in the book of James, but I read from the "Song of Solomon" for the steamy passages. I always get a kick out of the twin-mountain metaphors.

The service ends in song, and there is much rejoicing. I can smell the rosemary quiche from here. As Nora and I file outside, a woman in a navy sundress with a pink hockey-stick pattern squeezes my arm, too tight.

"Hi, are you Charlie?" She sounds like she's from the DMV. I've never seen whiter teeth on a human being in my life.

"Yes."

"Maugham's friend?" She squints her eyes at Nora. Maybe something *is* up. You only ever see something like this at the airport, when something's up.

"Yes, we're friends of Maugham's," Nora responds.

I haven't seen him today. I hope he didn't die or anything.

"If you could follow me through the back, Pastor Grey would like a word."

We follow the lady through a yellow curtain and down a hall of prayer rooms. Nora's lips tighten to a slit. She gets nervous easily. In fight-or-flight scenarios, she eats.

This Chick-fil-A corporal brings us into a prayer room. Cheap metal chairs from the '90s surround a plastic folding table. The room has that classic church smell: hand sanitizer meets antique shop.

"Have a seat. Pastor Grey will be in shortly." She takes a seat herself. We stare at different parts of the fascinating table.

"So, Maugham invited you over when? Last year?"

"Last month," I say.

"Very nice. And you?" She gestures at Nora.

"Last week."

"Very nice, very nice." All smiles so far.

The door opens, and three men march in, one of them the bald Pastor Grey.

"Charlie?" He has a tense slit between his eyebrows, a sort of yuppie sternness, like a guy with a high-pitched voice trying to speak in a baritone.

"That's me. They never found me in 'Nam." The joke whizzes right by everyone.

He squints at Nora. "And you are . . . ?"

"Nora," she announces, like a soldier.

Pastor Grey sits across from us, his fingers interlaced, and two unknown minions sit beside him, their fingers also interlaced.

This suddenly feels like a TSA interview. I interlace my fingers to counterattack.

"I called you both in here today to talk about a disturbing development in our church," the pastor says. "It seems that Maugham, a passionate member of the church, has left the church."

I hear the leather of Nora's shoes stretch from her curling toes.

"Left?" I clarify. "As in, quit?"

The council nods in unison.

"Did he mention why?"

"He wrote a letter," Pastor Grey snaps. "Obviously this comes as a complete shock to us, and we are all very saddened by Maugham's exodus."

That part sounds memorized.

"Maugham has renounced the church, renounced his faith, and claims he doesn't need either. However, I believe I know where this is coming from, and I'm afraid it involves you both."

A pregnant pause fills the room. In the distance, I hear someone playing rock and roll on the organ, but I can't make out the tune.

"Last Sunday, as we gathered for brunch, I overheard you having a rather disturbing theological discussion with Maugham."

I know exactly where this is going. I can predict the rest. We talked Maugham out of his religion, causing him to doubt himself and his faith, and we are not a good influence on the church, so unfortunately . . .

"So unfortunately, we don't see you as sincere members of the faith, and we are going to ask you both to leave until you have proven a sincere and honest conviction for the gospel. Do you have anything to say?"

Boy, is he mad. I can make out a throbbing vein on his bald head. If I were his ex-wife, I wouldn't want to wake up to that either.

Of course, we have nothing to say.

The organ player plays "Great Balls of Fire."

"You know if hell is real, we're toast, right?" I tell Nora. We march back to Harvard Yard in shame, under a light sleet, starving. "On the upside, I wouldn't need to spend eternity with Saddam Hussein."

"Don't make fun of this so much, I'm serious," she says.

"I'm not. I don't knock any religion. Any one of them might be true."

"I don't care what they say," she says, "no one abandons their faith after one conversation. Mother—Maugham—whatever his name is, he had to have been feeling agnosticky for a while."

"What are you talking about? He was so gung-ho, he deserves his own book in the Bible. If you didn't bring up that stuff about God lifting weights, we wouldn't be here."

"We have to call him," she says.

"And say what, reconvert yourself so we can eat?"

"Why else?" Now she's getting mad. Hangry is contagious.

We run into Tatte Bakery on Massachusetts Avenue, an overpriced French café. We are broke, but we're not animals; we won't submit to the dining hall yet. Our shoes squeak as we seat ourselves next to a man playing chess by himself.

"Do you want to talk to him?" I dial Maugham's number.

Nora shakes her head, drying her forehead with a napkin. I hear five rings.

"Hey, Charlie?"

"Maugham, hello, it's Charlie." I never know what to say on the phone. "Listen, are you busy right now?"

"Well, no, but I will be later. What's up?"

"Well, Nora and I are here at Tatte—"

"Hi, Nora!"

I put the phone on speaker. "He said, 'Hi, Nora.'"

"Oh, yes . . . hello, Maugham."

"Hi, Nora!"

"Hi, Maugham."

"We were just wondering, Maugham, why you weren't at church today . . ."

Nora validates this approach with an affirming look.

"Oh, yeah, that . . ." he starts. Does he know we know? "It's a bit of a long story, honestly."

"We love long stories," I say quickly.

"Well, okay." He takes a deep breath. "I left the church, guys. I know it seems like this happened all at once, but I've done a lot of thinking, and this just feels like the right next move."

I give Nora the "sounds wobbly" sign. She gives me what I interpret as the "squeezing a lemon" sign. I give her the "I'm confused" sign. She does what looks like the "YMCA" gestures.

"Look, Maugham, I hope this isn't about that conversation we had last week, about God building a weight he couldn't bench press or something."

"Oh no, it's not," he says. "Well it is, but it's not."

Nora winces.

"Honestly, I felt it was just time. I don't know. Yeah, it was just time."

His phone shakes and then is still. I can tell he just sat down.

"I come from a unique background that you wouldn't understand," he continues. "I was religious. Like, very religious. When you're raised like that, you don't know another way to exist. Then you travel somewhere, and you realize that there aren't people 'out to get you.' There aren't people trying to wreck your way of life because they don't care enough about you to wreck it. Living is hard, no matter who you are. Most everyone just wants their own version of *Friends*. Do you watch *Friends*?"

"Yes." My tone is soothing to keep him talking.

"Well, my *Friends* group was the church. Nothing else mattered, or even existed, as far as I knew. Do you see what I'm getting at here?"

I look at Nora for any ideas. She shakes her head.

"We hear you, Maugham. We get what you're saying, but we also don't," says Nora.

"It wasn't sudden. It started at university. It doesn't even feel like I'm leaving the church, it feels like I'm letting it go. A natural fade-out. That conversation we had last week was just a reminder of where I was. And the gym."

"The what?"

"Your gym membership. It filled that empty space, you know?"

"Maugham, you can't just phase out religions like Apple products. What about the prayers, the food, the community? The food?"

"Don't get me wrong, you and Nora should keep going."

Ironic. He is like everybody else in the end, and perhaps my mistake was imagining he wasn't. He is born from those delicate ingredients that make up untraveled boys who become men. When you change that mixture, add money, subtract it, find ambition and sex, fail, the whole dish changes. Then all preconceived notions of morality vanish like fog. Someone like that was bound to change gods eventually.

I've reconsidered stealing since the church expulsion. If you steal because of hunger, the crime is explainable to both a cop and a future employer. Maybe hunger is good for you, as Hemingway said, but Ernest never tasted this quiche. Nora feels tortured under her new, cheap living conditions. Yesterday she swore she'd rather starve than eat from the dining hall, and I thought she was joking.

Maugham wouldn't budge. After the third call, he stopped taking them.

We've tried a Wednesday service with the Unitarians, who have plenty of progressive ideas, but their meals are microwaved. I hear the Mormons don't serve coffee or tea, making it impossible to stay awake for their service. The Muslims let us cameo one Ramadan Friday, but it was too much of a hassle with the bowing and the head covering. When the Jews realized we were gentiles, they wouldn't even let us in the synagogue. They said they were "cleaning" that day.

We are out of ideas.

On Saturday I meet Mike at Grendel's Den, and he orders another milkshake, a sure sign that emotional woes are about to be gifted to me.

"The fight club isn't for me," he says.

"Is that what they said?"

"They said I'm a biter, not a fighter. And they're right. I kept biting guys."

I give this sentence a moment to digest. "Mike, why were you biting people?"

"My muscles haven't fully ripened yet. My jaw muscles are the only ones that can match a rear naked choke. I'm confused about this mentality of 'Do anything to survive, except everything we don't teach you.' You'd bite a guy to survive, wouldn't you?"

We share the milkshake with two fully platonic straws. I commiserate with him about what a terrible feeling it is, being dumped. I do the whole "it's their loss, not yours" routine. I also tell him about my church woes and how I can't get free meals anymore because of Maugham.

"You deconverted that kid?" he asks.

"He did say we were the tipping point." I say this like it makes any difference.

"You pagan sonuvabitch! You realize how much strife you've caused?"

"Why? He seemed happy. It's like he came out of the CrossFit closet."

"What about his family? His parents? He'll be stoned to death."

"Look, you've never even met the guy, and you're already making assumptions about his family?"

"You're right." He clasps his hands together.

"Shame be upon you, assuming he's happy." I don't

mean this, I just want to Uno reverse that Irish guilt of Mike's.

"Do me a favor and grab the ketchup from the other table, will you?" he asks.

I reach for the ketchup behind me, and for some reason, I see this as my golden opportunity to strike.

"Say, Mike, could you do me a favor back?"

"Sure."

"I need you to accept the Lord Jesus Christ as your savior."

He stops chewing. "What?"

"Not forever, just every Sunday from eleven to one," I clarify.

"Why the hell would I do that?"

"Well, you know, I do you a favor, you do me one."

"You passed the ketchup."

"All sins are equal in the eyes of the Lord, why can't all favors be equal?"

"Forget it."

"C'mon, I scratch your back, you bite mine?"

"Charlie, these are totally unequal favors. It's ketchup versus God. Where's this coming from? What are you, religious now?"

"No, I'm hungry now! It's that quiche, damn it! I can't live without it, and I'm fed up with these watery dining-hall eggs. Now be a pal and praise the Lord."

"But why do you need me there?"

"If you come, pretending like we converted you, the church will surely let us back in."

"Drop it. I'm not disrespecting a religious institution so you and Nora can pig out on MSG quiche."

"Mike, please, I need this. I haven't lain with a woman in weeks. This quiche is all I've got going for me this semester."

He looks at me, his expression changing from surprised to concerned. "I'm going. You get the check."

"Mike . . ." I grab his wrist. "I'm putting it all on the line here. I'm being vulnerable. You know what it's like to be kicked out of the boys' club, don't you?"

"This is different. You broke the rules. You break the rules, you're out. Plain and simple."

"You're telling me it doesn't feel even a little good to let others do your thinking for you? You just gotta sit there and be. No grades, no sales receipts—just be. That's what I'm getting at here. I got kicked out, and you're my ticket back."

He rubs his forehead with one hand. "But isn't it immoral?"

"That's what friends do, they commit sins together." A few tables have stopped talking and given us their chewing attention.

Mike fidgets with his lips. He clicks his nails when he's nervous, so I guess he fidgets with his lips when he's thinking.

Droplets of sweat slide down his iced water cup. He takes a
large gulp that leaves him lightly panting by the end. Somewhere in there, my barrage of words must have found their
way to him.

"All right," he says. "All right, I'll do it."

Nora and I wait outside Dunster House for Mike. I tell her
what a marvelous job I did last night selling him on the Lord.
She is proud but hungry and doesn't care. Unlike Mike, I
always had the lonely advantage of never being a part of a
group I needed to please. I'm too much of a jerk to be invited,
and because I'm not invited, I get resentful, which makes me
more of a jerk, making me more uninviting.

Mike comes down in a beige suit under his parka. He
doesn't look nervous at all.

"When did he drag you into this?" he asks Nora.

"I know how it looks," she says. "But this brunch will
change your mind. It'll change everything."

We take the train to Central. We must give our home-
coming prince the VIP experience. A man in an orange
construction uniform announces to the commuters that he's
been fired and proceeds to urinate on the floor. Only those
familiar with the "floor is lava" game survive the trickle. Nora
and Mike evidently never played.

We leave Central station and walk to church. No matter

what time of day, Central Square is filled with people in a daze. The mostly nocturnal nature of Central gives it an out-of-place feeling when the sun comes up. Something about Nora's and my mission not to pay for food turned personal, as most missions do. A trance; a personal crusade.

Again the bell rings as we arrive. Like Pavlov's dogs, I've associated it with feeding time and get hungrier at the sound.

The emcee is all congenial until he recognizes us. I grab a pamphlet out of his hand before he can reject me.

"Here." I shove it into Mike's hands. "Read up."

The Chick-fil-A lady welcomes people at the entrance of the main hall. She hasn't seen us yet. When I approach her with a phony, welcoming look, her phony look doesn't vanish like the emcee's, but she blinks at me.

"What a surprise," she says through a nervous nose-giggle.

"I know, right?" I open my palms as if I'm as surprised as she is, but she takes this as an invitation to hug. By the time I realize what she's doing, our heads turn the same direction and our lips peck. No one acknowledges what happened. I think the idea is, if you pretend long enough, it never happened.

"We are looking to speak with Pastor Grey—"

"I think that would be best." Chick-fil-A cuts me off and motions us to follow her.

She escorts us around some old church folks with flowers

in their hats and important expressions on their faces. I see the shine of the bald pastor shaking hands with a few of the congregation. He wears a plaid tie. Our escort whispers something in one of his pointy ears, and I see his neck tense. He glances at us, turns back around for one more grinning greeting, and then walks out a side exit. Chick-fil-A motions us to follow. We go through the same side door, and Pastor Grey stands with hands on his hips like Superman.

"Can I help you?" he asks, manager-style.

"Pastor Grey," I start. "Nora would like to apologize for the terrible thing she did, deconverting Maugham."

"It was never *our* intention," Nora adds. "In fact, I wanted to convert him even more."

"Yes, in fact, I felt he was too moderate," I say. "He only believed in the New King James version of God, and not the Old King James version. I encouraged the New Living Translation, but Maugham insisted on those free hotel Bibles, which I actually learned were not free."

"Sorry," Pastor Grey interrupts. "Is there something you wanted to speak with me about?"

"What we're trying to say," I continue, "is that even though things didn't work out with Maugham, we have been unwavering in our conviction for the gospel. I mean, we're just full of beans about it."

"Even though you have given up on us . . ." Nora gives

this a beautiful, guilt-packed pause. "We have not given up on God. Which is why we brought Michael today."

Mike offers a stiff wave.

"Michael accepted the Lord yesterday," I say, "but I wasn't sure if the Lord accepted Michael. I wanted to check with you."

Pastor Grey's face is slightly flushed, but his lips are slit shut. He offers his hand to Mike.

"Michael." He briefly acknowledges me and Nora with a subtle curl at the corner of his mouth. "Welcome."

We're in.

Mike, Nora, and I sit on the same bench during the service. As the youth pastor gets up there with the opening act, my mind dozes off. I catch myself drifting to sleep and straighten my spine, but soon I'm dozing again. The youth pastor is talking about hens and cocks as some kind of metaphor. I'm half conscious, but I can still hear him. And then I'm not.

I'm somewhere else entirely.

I'm in an elevator. Someone is with me, a guy about my age wearing a bucket hat and cargo shorts. He introduces himself as "Jat." The elevator is an old one. It squeaks like crazy, but I can't tell if it's going up or down. We don't say anything to each other. For some reason I can recall my whole life up to this elevator ride, but it's not my life, it's some other one, a biblically perfect life. All the times I'd been tempted,

I overcame them. Each time I had a chance to do the right thing, I did it.

The elevator stops, and we enter an empty conference room. Lilacs and Post-it notes clutter the middle of a modern conference table. A man in a suit sits in the middle of the table eating a salad. With a mouthful, he gestures us in with his fork but goes back to what looks like a crossword puzzle.

"Yo, you know where we're at, bro?" Jat asks me. He speaks two paces behind the beat.

"Do you remember anything before this?" I ask, because I don't.

"All I remember is dying, bro. I got hit by my own Uber."

A door opens and white light bursts through. A chorus of horns and a choir sing what sounds like an A note. A woman in a business suit and high heels enters, fixated on a file folder, not looking up at us. When the door shuts behind her, the light, the horns, and the chorus are abruptly muted. She sits down and sniffles, staring over her folder. The door opens again, with the light, chorus, and horns all starting up again, then shutting down when the door shuts. We are joined by an overweight man in a short-sleeved white shirt and tie, lugging a gallon of water that he clunks onto the table. They all sit on one side of the table, like the *Last Supper* but also like judges in a beauty contest. Nine vacant swivel chairs remain.

Jat says, "Whoa."

The first man, the one eating the salad, looks around. "Does anyone know where the others are? Will they be joining us?"

The other two shrug.

"Okay, I think we can get started then. Does everyone have their files?"

The other two grunt, not looking up.

"Let's begin." Salad Man looks at me. "Congratulations, you are dead."

"Is this heaven?" I ask.

"This is the documentation center, so almost. We review your lives and see if you are worthy to live in His eternal Kingdom of glory."

I remember my life, which flashes by in one second. It was a hard life, full of pain and restraint, but an intensely religious one. I have nothing to worry about, but somehow, I'm still perspiring under my arms.

"But where is God?" I ask. "I thought he judges me."

"You boys died during lunch hour, so not everyone's back yet."

"He's out to lunch?" I clarify.

"Don't worry. If you're approved, you can set an appointment to see him."

"But there's only three of you back from lunch. Is that enough to judge my life?"

Salad Man ignores this and bites into a brownie.

"So, Charlie, everything seems in order here, I'm not seeing any irregularities. Anyone else?" He glances to his sides.

The other two shake their heads.

"You made one joke about the Lord back in December, but I think we can overlook that."

"Oh, thank you," I say.

"Other than that, your file looks good. All those in favor of Charlie entering the Kingdom of God, say 'aye.'"

The three judges mumble a monotone "aye." Salad Man stamps a file.

"That's it?" I ask.

"That's all."

"I thought it would be more formal."

Salad Man shrugs. "Now, as for you, Jat . . ." He frowns at the name. "Am I pronouncing that right? J-A-T, Jat?"

"You got it, man," Jat responds, unusually relaxed.

"We're seeing here that you've lived an indulgent, hedonistic life. Much of your nineteen years was spent at parties, am I correct?"

"Yeah." Jat giggles with pride.

"Unfortunately that hedonism came with many sins."

The other two nod in unison.

"Atheism, idolatry, dishonesty, blasphemy, and recently you stole a lighter?"

"A couple, actually," Jat says.

"Oh, yes, I stand corrected." Salad Man straightens his tie. "But it looks like, in the last twenty minutes of your life, actually, you gave your life to the Lord?"

"Yeah, the Uber was picking me up from the church."

"Very good. I'm sure that was exhilarating."

"Oh, it was awesome. They dunked me in tap water and everything."

"A baptism!" Salad Man looks pleased. "Well, that does it for me. All those in favor of Jat entering the Kingdom of God, say 'aye.'"

Before he finishes, the other two judges say, "Aye."

"Awesome, bro." Jat does the "rock on" symbol.

"Hang on," I say. "I'm sorry to interject here, but *he* gets in?"

"Correct."

"How? You just said he lived a sinful life full of parties and one-night stands."

"But he gave his life to the Lord, in the end."

"In the last twenty minutes? He lived a good life for one *Friends* episode, and now he's in?"

"Well, yes, the Lord absolves all sins if you accept him."

"But this guy only accepted God at the very end, and he has a goatee. I lived almost sinless."

"I'm sorry, were you under the impression that life is a point system?"

The other two snort at this.

"Are you telling me I could have lived like him?" I ask. "Given in to every temptation and then, at the very end, I just give my life to God and I'm in?"

"It doesn't quite work like that. Jat never knew any better. You did. Planned redemption is no redemption at all."

"Then what was the point of trying?"

"You helped others. Didn't that feel good?"

"Well sure, but some adultery every now and then would've been great." I feel a sudden sadness. Anger mixed with sadness, creating a cocktail of resentment.

"Charlie, I know what you're trying to say here." Salad Man gently shuts his eyes and interlaces his fingers. That gesture feels familiar somehow. "The fact is, you're here, you've made it."

"But it doesn't make sense." Even in death, my life doesn't make sense. "If I knew this, I wouldn't have worked so hard."

Salad Man smiles. "They all say that."

Then I wake up.

Nora gently pats my cheek off of her shoulder. The organ is playing some worship tune, and the congregation, rising to its feet, makes the same sound as a hundred books tumbling off the shelf. I'm up. The singing begins, and I mumble-sing my way back to reality. As we sing, the tithing credit-card reader goes around. The man sitting next to me gives five dollars and hands it to me with a creepy grin. I hand it to Nora. She hands it to Mike. Mike puts his card in there and enters $50.

I grab his shoulder. "Mike, don't worry, you don't have to—"

"It's okay, Charlie," he assures me.

The last time I saw him with this kind of warmth, he was infatuated with a Yale shot-putter.

Nora touches his arm with an "Are you okay, should I call the police?" expression.

"I'm fine." He hugs her, and then me, and then the old lady beside him who didn't want to be hugged. He raises his hands and sways to the worship song. People give him approving slaps on the back.

What the hell happened here? I turn to Nora but she looks just as clueless as I feel.

"Praise the Lord . . ." the youth pastor purrs into the microphone. "Brunch will be served momentarily, so please praise the Lord in the dining hall, not in here. Thank you."

The congregation shuffles down the hall as the organ plays an outro with some blues notes that draw scolding looks from the older faces.

"Mike, are you okay?" I ask him. "You need an aspirin, Tylenol, morphine . . ."

"I'm fine." He restrains some internal joy that leaks out of his eyes. "Everything I ever worried about, even things I will worry about, I feel okay about them. I feel great."

He doesn't look great. Even I can admit it's a dopamine shot to sing those songs and pray those words, but I thought religious results like these happen only in the movies. As long as I've known him, there have been many versions of Mike, and I'm not sure I like Disciple Mike. Some people are more fun as alcoholic agnostics.

I can smell the rosemary outside, so I don't bring up Mike's awakening just yet. We're almost there, to do what we came to do. Even if part of me feels that familiar guilt for this phony religious routine, Nora and I are survivors, and there can be no apology for that. My mother always said, "If you don't survive, you won't be alive to apologize for it."

We find a seat near the fireplace, this time with some of the younger members of the congregation. No one talks religion once the service is done. That's usually how it goes, for some reason. The youth pastor invites someone to bless the food we are about to gorge down. I've always wondered what people think about during group prayers. Are you supposed to think about what's being prayed about or recite your own prayer? I don't know. With an "amen," we're unleashed. I grab a plate and pile it up. Nora follows, leaving a gap of three people to ward off suspicion between the unusually large portions. We have it worked out where she gathers the carbs, I gather the protein, and we divvy up later. We return to the table and soon Mike follows. I give him a Tupperware.

He acts like he has no idea what we're doing.

"This is how it works." I discretely slide chunks of meat-loaf into the container. "Now pack up before others get here."

"If you eat fast enough, you can go back for seconds," Nora adds.

"Wait a minute, guys. No," Mike announces. "I can't do this."

Me and the crew at NASA have this in common: we never want to hear these words before showtime.

"Why is that, Michael?" I use his full name, hoping to invoke some traumatic parental button of obedience.

"This is wrong. I'm not doing this, and you shouldn't, either."

"What are you talking about? This is why we're here."

"You're taking advantage of these people. You're telling me you felt nothing after that service?"

"I felt hungry."

"So do I, spiritually hungry."

"Mike, what the hell, you've been here for ninety minutes and now you're Billy Graham?"

"It's not right. I like these people."

"So do I. Their cooking is exquisite."

"Look, Michael." Nora uses his full name more effectively. "If it's not us, it's someone else. It's really a service that we're doing. At least the church can be screwed by decent people."

"Faking your faith for food doesn't make us decent," he says.

"Then what do you suggest, that we turn ourselves in?" she asks.

"Yes, that's exactly what we should do."

The quiche balances on my fork, and suddenly I feel a sick feeling in my gut like everything is about to go terribly wrong. "Mike, buddy, let's talk about this."

"What's there to discuss? I feel like I finally found a community that'll accept me—a family. Family is everything."

"Will you stop Vin Dieseling me with this crap? You're freaking me out."

"You never take anything seriously, not even me. Maybe that's why I feel this way. Did you ever think of that?" His voice is tinged with a threatening temper.

"Michael, you know what's going to happen? Let me tell you how this story ends." Nora sets down her spork. "They're going to honeymoon you for six weeks. Once you make friends, fall in love, maybe, and the rituals become habit, they start asking questions. They're going to feel out your belief system. If anything is out of line, that's when it begins. A mentor stops giving you attention. You don't get invited to a birthday party. A rumor goes around about you. You are slowly ignored, and that attention never comes back until you button up and become exactly who they want you to become. Once you do, the rumors magically go away. You're invited back to parties. People shake your hand. All until they start asking questions again. They don't stop. This is what they do. It's probably not intentional, even. It just happens to be this way."

Mike's face is still. I can tell he's thinking as his eyes travel across the table. He stands up and takes a deep, dramatic breath. "I'll say what I need to say."

He walks away, disappearing into the church.

Evidently nowhere in the Bible does it say "Thou shalt not tattle," because five minutes later, Chick-fil-A lady comes out. She calmly approaches us with the demeanor of a pre-school teacher and demands that we please leave the premises, or else she will contact the Cambridge Police for trespassing.

I had always assumed that Nora's suspicion of churches, and her one-toe-in attitude about religion, was the Catholicism talking. I ask her about it on our walk of shame back to Harvard Square, and she mentions only a distant friend who brought her into a church once, but she doesn't want to talk about it, so I let it go.

We make bets on how long Mike will stay in the church. Religion is an easy target, so everything we can say about it has already been said. Aristotle thought it was all about the truth—hell, Harvard says it's all about the truth, with that "veritas" jazz—but Nora says you can't make love to the truth, and she has a point. Honesty gets you killed, caught, and canceled. Eventually, life is all mapped out by relationships, and if that's the case, maybe Mike isn't so wrong, blending into solidarity. Besides, he had it rough in the romance department this semester. He was one rejection away from thinking Andrew Tate had some interesting points.

We walk back to Nora's dorm and eat crackers and hummus with cheap wine. We watch *Double Indemnity*. It is warm here, away from the rain, with a friend, and we forget about losing for a while.

One week later I hear that Mike has been accepted into a finals club, the Phoenix. Finals clubs are the fraternal tribes at Harvard; their esteem lies in their exclusivity: invite-only, with only about fifty members at a time. I don't know how the hell he got in, but he passed the initiation rituals and got the handshake. He skipped church, to celebrate, I guess. A week after that, he skips again, and then one day he isn't going anymore.

Nora manages a cease-fire with her family in Montreal. Once peace is restored, her checking account is liberated, and she calls me up to celebrate. We arrange a solid old-money meal at Grafton Street with oysters and lobster.

We sit near the window on the last day we can, I think,

since the Boston winter is next in line, and even tempered glass does little to stop that windy bite. We eat calamari and talk about whether art needs pain to survive. The waitress lights a candle at our table and Chet Baker's "Deep in a Dream" plays from the speakers.

A passing figure on the sidewalk stops at our table.

"Charlie? Nora?"

It's Mike. With a guy like Mike, he'll just pick up from where you last left off and act like nothing happened. He displays his new finals club ring and tells us where he plans on going during winter break. I can see he is happy. He no longer carries a perpetual stillness in his lips.

"What's happening here?" Ted's familiar voice approaches our table, parking what looks like a recently invented scooter by the coats. He reaches over and steals a fry from Nora's plate.

"Pull up some chairs," Nora says. "Eat with us."

"I was on my way to dinner with someone," says Mike.

"Cancel it. Eat with us."

"All right." He shrugs.

Ted doesn't even try to resist. The moment Nora speaks the invitation, he drags a vacant chair from an occupied table.

"Isn't this nice?" Nora comments as they sit. "Tell me this isn't beautiful."

"I'm thinking of starting a pyramid scheme," says Ted.

"You don't have better hobbies?" she asks.

"Well, apparently therapy isn't a hobby."

"Who told you that?"

"My therapist."

The waitress arrives and draws her pen. "Are you all ready to order?"

"Would you recommend the chicken Kiev? No, never mind. That's what I'll have," Nora says.

"I'll have the lobster bisque," Mike says this with a finger pointed haughtily up.

"Bison burger. Medium rare," Ted quips.

"I'll have scrambled eggs," I say.

They look at me.

"For dinner?" Nora's eyebrows arch.

"Yes."

"What if it's all watery?"

"Right now, it couldn't matter less."

I breathe in the night. Yes. This is nice.

looking for love in a loveless world

(december)

I'm through with love. It's over. December 14, 8:03 p.m. An addict must see his dependency with honest, unblinking eyes eventually. I'm a serial dater, an addict of love and dating and romance. Well, it's all over, starting now.

The moment I finish writing these words, a girl steps into the café, out of breath. She removes a coat and shakes her enormous, dark, curly hair from a long neck. It is the beginning of every boy-meets-girl rom-com the '90s spat out like carbon dioxide. I'm writing a finals essay called "Mr. Stalin Goes to Washington" to continue justifying my confused presence at college, and in she walks. My latency period rebooted. It is best to avoid cliché, whether in fiction or reality, so I swallow my attraction and stare at the cursor on my screen.

A relaxed, almost husky tenor asks if the seat next to me is open. She didn't need to ask, but she did anyway. Interesting.

"Of course, sure." I unnecessarily move a napkin, as if that were in her way.

She sets up camp right beside me, shoulder to shoulder, close enough to see what the other is writing. She smells like fresh coconuts. Our elbows, within millimeters of each other, almost kiss. I feel the heat emitting from her forearms on mine. I can clearly feel something about to happen, that feeling of reaching the final three pages of a long novel, the seconds before stepping onto a plane, or the desire to talk to a beautiful stranger.

"Say," she announces after about ten minutes. "I'm going to order something. Could you watch my stuff?"

"Sure."

"And if anyone tries to steal it, you know . . ." She makes a gesture with her head as if it should be obvious. "Get two or three jabs in, but go for the takedown early, get them on the ground." She demonstrates the method she expects me to employ. "And if they keep struggling—triangle choke until submission. Got it?"

I laugh at this mild joke, and she smiles, a sparkling, particular smile, until she suddenly goes dead serious, looking me straight in the face as if terrible news is coming. This makes me go dead serious, and we study each other's dead-serious faces for a few seconds, long enough for people to notice, until she breaks into a quiet giggle.

"Oh." I laugh it off, too.

"Sorry, I'm horrible at jokes. I act strange when I'm nervous."

"No, that was perfect. You don't have to feel nervous."

"I kind of do." She stretches her fingers briefly. "You're all-right-looking, and when I saw you, I said to myself, 'Oh . . . right.' That's why I sat next to you."

Fellow café patrons give us the glances. "Really, that's what you really thought?" I ask, straightening my glasses. "I was attracted to you, too, when you walked in, but I just didn't know that you . . ."

"Would you have said something to me if I didn't walk up?" she asks.

"Would you have wanted me to say something?" I ask.

"Do you always answer a question with a question?"

"Do I?"

"You've never noticed?"

"Should I have noticed? Does it bother you?"

She starts laughing through her lines. "Should it bother me?"

"If not you, then who should it bother?"

"What was the question again?"

"The question was, would you like to sip some apple cider together?" I ask.

The corners of her eyes slightly narrow, as if she's smiling without her lips.

We talk over hot apple ciders. The café plays Benny Goodman's "Where or When," and it puts us in this warm, dreamy state of mind. What's more is she's a marvelous conversationalist. We put away our textbooks—with conversations like this, studying loses importance. I don't think either of us even knows what the hell we're talking about. It's like that, pointless but nice.

When I ask for her number, she does that thing girlfriends do where they casually change the subject and make it look like it was your idea. When I bring it up again, she says I ought to read her favorite book and then "find" her again.

I pause. "*Find* you again? What is this, a Hugh Grant movie?"

"You don't know me; I don't know you. Isn't this a good way to know each other?"

"Well, yeah, but so is this, us talking."

"You've clearly never been in love with charming European men." She even sips her cider nice. "I hate being a princess about this, but this is just the way I've decided to do things."

"What is it, like a test to ward off the lazy guys?"

"It's just my style."

"So I've got to read this whole book to see you again?"

"That is correct," she answers.

"What is it called?"

"*Love in a Loveless World.*"

I stare in disbelief. "Can't I just wait for the movie to come out?"

She grins again, almost to herself, and stands up, packing her bag.

"Will a CliffsNotes do?" I try again. "What's your name?"

"Diane."

"Diane what?"

"Diane Nice Try But You're Not Going to Look Me Up on Socials." She puts the backpack on.

"You're going to exist in my head as Diane Something."

"Fine."

"All right, Diane Something, I'm Charlie."

"Goodnight, Charlie. Until we meet again, and I hope we do."

She doesn't look back when she walks out the door. I wait about seven seconds before I cup my hands to the cold window to see if she does look back, and as she crosses the street at the corner of JFK and Winthrop, just before her body disappears behind the red bricks, she does.

A CliffsNotes would not do, since no such thing existed for this book. Okay, she probably did this before with other guys, and they all failed. I'll prove her wrong.

I find the book at Widener Library, in the nightmarish basement three levels down. You must be careful not to interrupt a delicate moment down here, for it is a tradition for every Harvard student to get intimate in the bowels of Widener before graduating. I often hear the lovely noises of seniors getting busy, and I used to leave, but then I got used to it and even trained my ear to hear the fakers. Things got strange when I once heard my economics professor getting acquainted with my poetry professor down there. She wanted him to recite Proust during the act, but all he could do was sensuously sum up the national debt policy toward China in iambic pentameter. It sounded like they reached common ground.

I find *Love in a Loveless World* collecting dust in the psychology section, and I skim through the beginning of the four-hundred-page bastard.

The introduction presents the odds of finding "the one." The average human life is seventy-eight years. Assuming you meet or meaningfully interact with three *new* people a day, then on average, you will know 85,410 people in your lifetime. But let's say 10 percent are within your age range (up to five years difference), which brings that number down to 8,541, and if you're heterosexual (see page 158 for gay and bisexual odds), half that number is male or female, bringing it down to 4,270. The median age of marriage is 29.5 for men and 27.4 for women, so we assume the prime "soulmate find-ing" years are between 18 and 40. In that twenty-two-year window of prime searching, we apply the math and we get:

24,090 people met after twenty-two years

2,409 within age range

1,204 heterosexual

Divide that by twenty-two years, and you meet fifty-four potential mates a year. This does not take into consideration physical attractiveness or compatible personalities. Out of fifty-four people, how many do you find attractive? Assume it is half—twenty-seven. Of that number, how many also find *you* attractive? Assume two-thirds—eighteen. Of these eighteen potential partners, how many would you get along with? How many would be in your city? Or your country?

I stop reading. The sad part is I don't think I meet even fifty-four new people a year. Jesus. Do bisexuals double their odds? What a before-bed read. As I put this depressing thing in my backpack, I notice handwriting on the front flap. A wavy handwriting, written in purple ink.

Dear Reader: I guess that means we ought to fall in love any chance we get. Find your dance partner and that'll be your soulmate, I guess. But soulmates are hard to come by these days, especially in this economy.

I pull out a pen from my breast pocket and write just under this:

Life is too hard not to imagine the best is yet to come.

And then I reconsider taking the book with me. Maybe Diane Something wrote this, and it is her clever idea of communicating. I put the book back on the shelf with the silly idea that someone will read my entry and be inspired to believe that life still has lovely pages in it.

The next morning I study in the companionable silence of Lamont Library. My course on Nazi propaganda required me to watch a lot of Nazi propaganda over the semester. From a personal PR perspective, this can look exceptionally bad to someone standing behind me. I think I've publicly become "that guy" at Lamont who watches Nazi chick flicks all night.

In the background noise of my mind, thoughts of Diane Something's favorite book flicker like a broken screen. I wonder if, truly, it all ends in the dry world of practicality, if we all start young and moisturized and end up sunburned anyway.

At 1:36 p.m., after my History of Agnosticism class, I go back to the third-floor basement of Widener and check on the book. I don't know; I just have a feeling.

I run up the Rocky-esque stairs, scan my student ID, wave at the Widener security guard—the whole routine—and descend into the basement. I remember exactly where the book is. When I pull it out, I flip open the front flap, and there it is, a response:

We're all lost. But another animal with nowhere to go is out there roaming the streets of Boston, and that is what matters.

Diane Something has a poetic brain. It nudges my curiosity. I write, just under her entry:

Today I saw a pigeon break up with her boyfriend. He was having an affair with a duck.

I eat a croissant for lunch, with sparkling water and lemon, thinking about nothing for no particular reason. Not nothing, but the concept of nothing, how no one talks about it like they talk about infinity. Is nothing a place? Where does something go when it ceases to exist? People occupy only a swatch of time on earth before they return to nothing. That old cliché comes to mind, how we are born naked, confused, and in diapers, and then we die naked, confused, and in diapers. No way nature just does that—its sense of humor isn't *that* dark. Images like that make one believe in God.

The moment thoughts of mortality come into the picture, I cannot keep my eyes attached to my textbook on the mysteries of the hippocampus. What is the point if we're all doomed to nothingness? I don't care how we use our brains, the point is we use them, and no one knows the rest.

I write drafts on a napkin of what I will say next to Diane Something. And then, suddenly, I'm too bored even to do that. I run over to Widener, into the basement, and check on the book.

Under my last entry are the words:

Maybe the girl pigeon was seeing a goose on the side and the boy pigeon got jealous and had to prove himself by getting with a duck but deep down he still loves her.

So, I write back:

See I thought that too, but there must be a reason she felt the need to see a goose outside of her monogamous pigeon relationship. The truth is, their gratitude languages were mismatched. He likes giving her specks of bread from cafés. He likes receiving kisses on the beak. However, she likes watching people from on top of traffic lights with him and defecating on moving heads. She likes receiving acts of bravery, like fending off other pigeons. Their gratitude languages were off, they wanted to give and receive different things. When the language is off, everything is off.

I check back at Widener before dinner at 5:02 p.m. to see that she's written:

The girl pigeon was heartbroken. The goose, although he promised her a life of adventure in Canada, flew south for the winter and never called. She paced around in circles; she didn't care when kids ran up to her and tried to scare her. She hated life. She wanted to start all over, be a baby pigeon again.

I write:

The boy pigeon did not treat his new duck girlfriend right.
He would always make fun of her friends for having flat feet
and demean her religious beliefs as "pure quackery." The ugly
duckling did not understand why he treated her so. The fact is,
he was hurt—he could not understand himself. He flew around
looking for reasons to find food and he gained weight hanging
around the alley behind Dunkin' Donuts, picking off bits of
blueberry donut holes. He was a lost bird.

After dinner, I run back to Widener. I see she's written:

The girl pigeon needed help. She consoled a wise owl psy-
chic who was said to have been an extra in the last Harry Potter
movie. The owl had the pigeon imagine her death, the last few
moments of her pigeon life, and then how she would feel about
her ex-boyfriend. The pigeon had an epiphany—she still loved
her ex. She didn't want him to fly away. She wanted to fly with
him forever.

I write:

The boy pigeon came home to his duck girlfriend's nest by
the Charles one night and found that her duckling gal-pals had
given her a makeover and totally transformed her into a svelte,
swanlike duck. He was astonished. "Baby," he cried. "Don't
'baby' me you two-faced flying-rat. You never treated me right.
I'm a strong independent duck who don't need no pigeon to boss
her around." Her duckling friends quacked in agreement, and

*they all flew off to a nightclub called the Duck Pond. The pigeon
knew it was over. He left empty, alone, waddling to town with
traces of fallen feathers trailing him.*

In the morning at 8:16 a.m., I wake up thinking about her.
I gobble breakfast and run to Widener, half hoping to run
into her.

I find the book, snap it open, and read her entry:

*The girl pigeon flew aimlessly from stop sign to stop sign.
She went on one date with a seagull who looked like Jerry Mc-
Guire in his white uniform, but she felt no chemistry. She paced
around a rooftop, praying the boy pigeon would call . . .*

I guess this is my cue. I write:

*The boy pigeon bottled up his emotions and by the thirti-
eth time he watched* Top Gun, *he knew it was time to call. He
couldn't take it anymore. He called her:*

"Hello?"

*"Darling," he cried. "I've been a bird-brain. I'm sorry for
everything. I love you."*

*"I love you too and don't be sorry. I'm one who should be
sorry for cheating on you with that goose. He done me wrong.
He flew to Alberta."*

"I'll break his neck when I see him."

*"I miss you," she says. "I don't want to wander this world,
defecating on windshields alone."*

"I miss you too. I want to flock back to you, if you'll have me. Let's meet, just name a place and I'll be there."

I snap the book shut and walk away.

Later that evening at 9:03 p.m., I ride the train to Central Square, one stop away from Harvard, for Thursday night jazz. Our band is so bad that one night, a Juilliard music professor called the police on us. The sign outside the bar says Live Jazz, but if they put Deceased Jazz it would avoid false advertising.

We play the classics: "All of Me," "Dancing in the Moonlight." The audience does not throw eggs, clearly a crowd of nonjazz lovers who don't know the difference between bad and awful.

We take the red line back to Harvard Square. On the way, a street preacher claims he's the genuine Jesus and he'll personally forgive our sins for three easy payments of $39.99. The yelling makes Ted hungry for Le's, a Vietnamese restaurant, and at first Mike isn't in the mood, but Ted's talking about it makes him hungry and he agrees. It is either this or I watch *Uncle Adolf* again. I go with them.

Le's glows a sunset warmth from cloth lanterns and steaming pho. It is home after a bad day—you can sit at the bar and forget about what's wrong over a coconut.

We shift our weight around the hard, contoured wooden seats and order coconut waters.

"I'm going to the bathroom, everyone." Ted always announces when he's going to the bathroom.

While I have Mike alone, I tell him about this library correspondence I've been having. He listens carefully and lets me finish the whole story of how I met her.

"What book was this?" he asks.

"Some BS psych book called *Love in a Loveless World.*"

"In the Widener basement?"

"Yeah. Why?"

After a beat of rare, vulnerable pondering, he says, "You know, it's probably one of the librarians."

In that moment, Ted sits back down. "What's one of the librarians? What'd I miss?"

"Nothing," I snap. I don't want Ted to hear—he'll for sure have some paranormal conspiracy theory. Besides, I can never be as raw with Ted. Some humor-driven defense mechanism always blocks us from going there.

"Charlie. New girl," Mike grunts.

"Checks out," Ted snickers.

They are good friends, but their intuitions assume the worst, either because of a subconscious desire to withhold happiness until they themselves are happy, or because bringing butterfly-filled friends back to earth is a moral duty of friendship.

"Your cynicism is appreciated, but I think she's someone special." I stretch my neck.

"You're not thinking, you're wishing," Mike says. "Big difference."

"Wishing? What, I think the worst of every possible situation in life, and then have the nerve to go wishing?"

"Bet you wish you weren't single," Ted snorts.

"Look, relationships all come down to compromise, don't they?" Mike says. "A game of how long you can stand each other."

"I don't believe that," I say. The coconut waters arrive. I poke at mine with a straw.

"You don't or you won't?" Mike sips his like it's a martini. "You can't ride this infatuation merry-go-round forever. You'll have a heart attack."

"Okay, so what's your point?"

"That you can't put all your money on love," he says. "You fall in love with the person they are, not the person they become. Kids, money problems, your parents getting old— it humbles everyone. People change, and often they change in ways that don't fit each other. You fall in love with one person and twenty years later—*boom*. They're someone else. Just hope you both change into people that get along with each other later. But of all the ways to end up being, I never liked the odds of that."

I crumble up the straw wrapper and flick it to ceiling. "I can't afford to think like that."

"Why not?"

"I just can't. Too much is wrong with the world, and I don't need simple affection to join that club."

"Forget it, Mike," Ted chimes in as our pho arrives. "When a guy falls, you can't save him halfway down. His whole belief system changes."

"All I'm saying is, look at what's wrong with the world," I say, tearing open the chopsticks. "It's all wired against us: we're brought into it without our consent, we get screwed with jobs we hate because the alternative is getting screwed with poverty. You have to get screwed to get enough money not to get screwed. The world screws you over eventually, so I think the best we can do is find someone to get screwed with."

Mike turns to Ted. "So, Freud was right. It all comes down to getting screwed."

I don't care what these geniuses think. They're single anyway. I am a harsh realist, but reality is cold. Fantasy is the blanket.

All that nihilistic dinner talk got me depressed. I am slinking on home when I realize I must check the book before Widener closes. The library is sprinkled with studiers, future doctors and lawyers and senators who will one day maintain the illusion of a civilized world. Funny to think that, right now, a future Supreme Court judge is just some guy named Jake.

I go to the basement, straight to the book. A couple is

getting it on a few shelves down, but boy is she faking it. I
open the book to find the purple cursive letters:

*The girl pigeon thought for a moment. Was she ready to do
it all over again? She would have to take that chance.*
*"Tomorrow night," she said. "10:30 p.m. The Kong restau-
rant. I'll be reading* The Invisible Man *by H.G. Wells and
listening to 'Both Sides Now' by Joni Mitchell."*

I wake up at Lamont in the Farnsworth room at 11:11 a.m. on
these sofas that are so plush I could die and nobody would notice
for a week. This is my kind of place, somewhere to disappear into
and not worry about people and their demands. I find a copy
of *The Invisible Man* and read the CliffsNotes so I can sound
well-read over lo mien and restless thoughts about humanity.

I try not to think about Diane Something. That way the
date will be natural, without expectations jinxing me out of
possibility. It is always about possibility—the possibility of
someone leaping into my life and resurrecting what I lost, rekindling the spark in me. All things good are about to return,
in the palm of her hands.

I study all day, like the discipline will bring me faster to
10:30 p.m. Life feels good again.

I wear a black suit, and I look writerly, like a man about to
make a breakthrough toward something he'd been trying to

understand for years. I go to CVS, steal a finger of pomade, and mold myself a hairdo. I even purchase a single white lilac. I don't know why a lilac, maybe I'll just say it reminded me of her.

At 10:41 p.m., I huff a fresh intake of air and walk into Hong Kong. "The Kong," as it is known among students, is a famous late-night hangout. The first floor is a homely Chinese restaurant with pleasant Chinese music. The second floor is a loud comedy club engineered to get you drunk on weeknights.

The Kong is a little empty tonight, only one waitress waiting six tables. Diane Something sits at none of them. I assume she is late, fashionable or not. I sit in a booth and order jasmine tea. Three tables down a man in a suit hums the Russian national anthem over crab Rangoon. He never once looks up from his meal.

The last occupied table in the back gives me pause. I missed it when I walked in, and I can only see a book blocking the face of the diner. I stand up with my lilac and walk over slowly. As I arrive, the book lowers to reveal the face of Ted in a white seersucker suit. He is reading *The Invisible Man*.

I do not have a heart condition, but I might be developing one.

"Are you—*with* Diane?" I ask.

"Charlie?" He glances at the lilac. "Who's Diane?"

"*The Invisible Man*," I say to myself aloud. "She said she would be reading *The Invisible Man*. But no, you're reading *The Invisible Man*, because you're not her. You're Ted."

His expression changes for the sour. "Hang on, you wrote in that library book?"

"Sure did."

"What is this?" His face gets red. "Look, man, I got my expectations up. How could you do this to me?"

"You think I would have kept writing if I knew it was you? You have some feminine handwriting, you sonuvabitch."

"The least you could have done is write your name," he jabs back.

"Hey, whoa, this goes both ways. The least you could have done is pick a different colored pen, okay? I mean, purple?"

"The least you could have done is not ask me to open up to you. It's just . . ." He starts weeping, out of nowhere, loudly. I've never seen Ted weep before, so I don't know what's real and what's a put-on. "You led me on."

The other diners are now gazing at this drama. I'm the bad guy, and Ted's the wounded; that's how this looks now. Beautiful.

"You're blaming *me* for your hurt feelings?" I challenge him. "How are you the victim here? I bought the flower. I got dressed up. I got my hopes up, just like you, pal."

"It's not the same thing!" He throws a fortune cookie at my face and it hits my glasses.

"It's exactly the same thing!" I whack the lilac into his cheek.

"No, it's not. I thought I was opening up to a confident, beautiful woman. But look at you, you've got hair like Moses!"

We are now yelling.

"Well, who do you expect someone to be, other than imperfect?" I say. "I mean, that's what it is, isn't it? Only wanting what you expected. I could have been anybody—I could have been Monica Bellucci for all you knew, and you'd still be upset because I am different from what you imagined. Why are *you* even crying? You're not even listening. *I* am the victim here!"

Our little Tennessee Williams scene is interrupted by the Cambridge Police. The manager must have called them. Two bored cops appear behind me and insist that we both leave the premises. I oblige, with enthusiasm.

"Look, fights happen, we get it," the officer tells me in his Boston accent, outside the restaurant. "But you and your partner need to keep them inside your residence."

"We're not together," I clarify.

"That's not the point here. You just can't be having relationship brawls inside public places, okay?"

"You don't understand. We are not a thing. We know each other, but I thought he was someone else."

"Yeah, I thought he was a hot babe," Ted snaps.

"Right, we both thought we were hot babes, which we are not, and now we hate each other for it. Simple mistake."

The officers give us a routine lecture about domestic violence and offer the phone numbers of a few therapists in the Cambridge area. They wish us goodnight and groan away into their squad car.

Ted crosses his arms bitterly. I'm guessing he feels especially alone. I can see this meant more to him than some bizarre misunderstanding.

"Look, Ted, I'm sorry. Let's just forget about this, okay? This is such a weird thing that happened here, but let's just be cool with each other. I don't want to run into you at the library and have this thing every time."

"It doesn't work like that. People say 'forget about it' all the time."

He gazes at the ground like the answers are there, and then starts walking. I follow. That cool metallic taste in the air whistles through the streets as a group of students waits, depressed, outside Widener Gate for the Quad shuttle. The Russian classical guitarist plays, even though it is December.

"Look, Ted, let's go to Tasty Burger and forget this whole thing. Man to man."

"Tasty Burger is too greasy."

"How about Grendel's, then?"

"I went there two nights ago." He continues to walk but doesn't turn me away. He wants to suffer alone, but he also wants a friend to feel alone with him. Maybe I do, too.

"Well, I don't know what's open at this hour, other than the Kong, but we're probably banned for life now."

"Zinneken's," he mumbles. "They're open."

We walk in that direction.

The clean, massive windows of Zinneken's reflect the moon, reeling you in from the cold. It is tiny, warm, and Belgian. It is lit like an art gallery. The waffles and coffee are the stuff of last meals. Places like these—Zinneken's and Mike's Pastry, Grafton Street and Tealuxe—they give Cambridge that lost European feel; a city displaced in time, free from the hurricane of real life.

We sit at a tight corner table next to a woman in a respirator face mask and a bucket hat. Ted is still sulking like a maniac. I no longer feel disappointed. Seeing someone worse off often cures vain sadness. It's hard being this open with him. I don't think we've ever discussed anything deeper than hockey and the weather.

"Look, Ted," I start, "if you want to know the truth, this mission to find someone isn't so noble."

"I don't think so," he says. "Only with the wrong people, maybe."

"But there are so many wrong people."

"That's why you have to find your exception."

"But that's what falling for someone is," I say. "We always think this next person is the exception, and they're just not."

"Well, what is the exception?" he asks.

I look out the window. "When you can take out your thoughts for someone, and you play catch with them awhile, knowing the other person won't ever drop them. People wonder why some people don't show themselves, their real selves, and I think it's because we toss it to too many people who don't catch it. But then, you find that one person, when you thought you'd never find them, and life is good again. You see what I'm getting at here?"

He stares over my shoulder, avoiding eye contact. "I'm hungry."

I go to the counter and order two banana-Nutella waffles with coffee from the happy waitress. Nothing is ever wrong with a Zinneken's waffle. When they are ready—golden and hot, glaciers of thick, real whipped cream cresting the center of each waffle, waiting to melt inside your warm mouth—I steal a bite. It feels like a kiss.

With the metal tray of steaming waffles and coffee, I turn around, and through the window I see Ted skipping off down Harvard Street.

Joni Mitchell's "Both Sides Now" plays in the café. It breaks my heart. I stand there as the song plays, feeling a thousand years old. Then I bring the Belgian feast to the table anyway, because—hell, I don't know.

But the night isn't over. At the corner table where the lady on the respirator and sunglasses sat is . . . Diane. She stares right through me, saying nothing. I say nothing back.

She says she likes this song. She likes this place, too. It is her favorite.

"Are banana-Nutella waffles your favorite?" I ask.

A calm look of satisfaction forms across her face. "Your friends, those two guys—they're a little strange, sorry."

"I know."

"They found the book in the library," she says. "They knew I'd be at the Kong, so they met me there before you came. They told me to come here and do all this. They said it was a prank, but I think it's the only way they can say they love you."

This makes me laugh. I could also cry, but I won't.

"He chose Zinneken's," she says. "But I couldn't be sure you would pick banana-Nutella. That was pure luck."

"This is my favorite song in the whole world," I say.

"What are the odds of that? Is that fate or chance?"

"Whatever it is, I'm beginning to believe we pigeons are a lot luckier than we think. Because amidst all that's wrong in this world of ours, still, somehow, we will always find a way to fall in love."

"So, what do we do now?" I ask her.

She smiles, gently. "We play catch."

walking home

(december)

The sirens inside Sever Hall last week were nothing serious.

A Harvard employee went on a date at the Daedalus restaurant the other night with a Sigourney Weaver–looking woman. The date did not go well, due to religious differences: he is an atheist, and she doesn't care what he is. He couldn't stand that. But when he opened his fortune cookie, the only redeeming crumb of the night, it said: "It is time to rekindle an old flame."

During work hours in Sever Hall, he tried rekindling this old flame through a love note, but deciding it was a bad idea halfway through, he literally kindled the rekindling note and threw it, while burning, in the waste bin. This did not end well.

I was in the basement bathroom when this happened. I went up to a urinal and saw, in my peripheral vision, an acquaintance from MIT named Pong at the adjacent urinal. I turned, and the instant I said, "Hi, Pong," the fire alarm went off. I heard loud groans in the stalls on my way out.

Students and staff panicked like they were already on fire. A lady wearing bell-bottoms held open the entrance, commanding everyone to "Be cool, be cool." I later learned she felt guilty about being publicly unkind to a maintenance worker that morning in the lobby, and it probably bothered her all morning, so she went into hyperkindness mode, looking for redeeming acts that would make her conscience stop pestering her. With the warning of an apparent fire, she hit the jackpot, and deep down I think she was hoping for snake eyes, someone trapped in the bathroom that she could rescue. She was getting kindness-greedy.

Hordes of students and faculty congregated outside Sever, staring at a third-floor window leaking smoke. I didn't see Pong, and I hope he wasn't trampled on. However, I did see Professor Bergman, the bearded Introduction to Philosophy professor. He got very emotional about the fire and began crying, for some reason.

About a week later, I accidentally overheard why he got so emotional.

I was at Grafton Street, arguing with Nora over whether the top at the end of *Inception* falls or keeps spinning, and as I sat there hating my life, I heard Professor Bergman in the booth behind me, going on about his childhood, how his parents owned a nursing home on a hill, overlooking a lake.

"And this one night, I'm about fifteen," I heard his open-throat voice pensively explain, "and I'm the only one on the night shift. I'm just watching television when pretty soon I smell smoke, and then a fire forms. I start rushing everyone out in their wheelchairs, as quick as I can, wheeling them outside and running back in to get more. I manage to get everyone out, but then they were gone, just like that. When the fire department came and put the fire out, the police searched the area for the bodies. They found them all right—all thirteen of them, in the lake, drowned. When I pushed them outside, as fast as I could, their wheelchairs went down the hill and into the water. I saved them from fire by drowning them."

A five-second hush went by before his date, I assume, replied, "So wait, your parents made you work when you were fifteen? Isn't that child labor?"

Every time I saw Professor Bergman after that night, I felt more understanding of his suffering, which oddly made me feel more understood. Trying to understand someone can have that effect. I came to see him as a friend, but he never reciprocated this feeling because he never knew I accidentally overheard him.

Whenever I saw him at Sever, I would say, "Hello, Professor Bergman. I hope you are well."

He would look up and say, "Oh, yeah, hello, Charlie. Good work on that final."

And I would thank him, hoping for more, but more never came. I wondered how many people in the world could even relate to my situation. And suddenly I felt very alone. But keeping secrets is a lonely pastime. Maybe on a rainy, do-nothing day when you dream about what you're going to become, a beautiful stranger could drift into your life and ask all your secrets, and you could ask them, "Why?" And they could say, "So that you won't be alone."

It is the end of another semester at Harvard. We are going home, to remember where we came from, and to beg our parents for more money.

Nora takes me, Mike, and Ted to dinner at Russell House Tavern. We eat clam pizza and talk about all the places we will go one day, when we are rich and happy. I cannot love endings, and I cannot hate them. What is worse than goodbyes is no goodbyes. I'll see them again in a few weeks, I know, but the ending of a chapter reminds you that this story must end, too. Sometimes endings just need a few moments of something: silence, one more word, one more kiss—something. Most goodbyes lack just one more thing.

"I'm going to miss this," I say.

"Miss what?" Ted asks, his fingers playing with two toothpicks.

"This. Being twenty. With you guys."

"The night isn't even over, and you're missing it already?" he asks.

"Sure. It keeps me sharp to recognize the good times while they're happening," I say.

"You're a nostalgia addict," Ted says. "A nostal-dict. That's you."

"If you feel nostalgic, I think that's a good thing," says Mike. "It means things have gone well so far. Nostalgia is life's way of saying keep up the good work."

The waiter brings out coffee and Boston cream pie. We take occasional sips and bites over conversation about endings and beginnings.

"Is it just me," starts Nora, sipping down her pompous after-dinner espresso, "or do we not make as many friends as we used to? There's this brain elasticity at eighteen that seems to harden with time. That elasticity isn't gone, we're still young, after all, but it's less, and I have a feeling it'll be gone for good at a certain age. Is it just me?"

"Nah, it's not just you. Me, too." Ted says this and offers no more context. He'd been drinking "grape juice" earlier.

"Parents, for instance," Nora continues. "My parents don't make new friends. Do yours?"

"Nope," says Mike. "They pick their tribe and that's it."

"A little sad," I say.

"It's not that sad if that's just the way it goes," Mike says. "Nothing tragic about nature."

"There's a lot that's tragic about nature," I say.

"No, there isn't."

"Sure there is. Dying is natural, and that's still tragic," I say.

"Not really."

"Yes, really."

"Dying is only a tragedy for the ones who live on." Mike leans in. "For the one dying, it doesn't matter, does it? They're dead."

I mention my theory, that our brain elasticity for discovering people to feel understood with has to do with beginnings. "It was nicer knowing what we weren't capable of," I say. "Because now we gotta wake up knowing what's possible."

"I still don't know what's possible," says Ted.

"It's probably simpler than that," Nora says. "I think friends become harder to find because we firmly decide who we become later in life. See, right now, college . . . no one knows who they are. We're all experimenting. You get to our parents' age, and you commit to being someone, that experimental spirit disappears."

"But you have to pick the person you're going to be eventually," Mike says. "We can't experiment forever."

"No," she replies. "But it's sure fun while it lasts, isn't it? Deciding who to be."

Out of nowhere, Ted's wine-drunk words speak his thoughts: "You know, I love you guys. You companions, you chums, compadres, fellow humans . . . friends are hard to come by. I thought I'd mention it in case we die one day."

Nora, Mike, and Ted slowly fade back home after dinner. No real deadlines remain, so students tend to stick around and then gradually leave without announcing it. I wind up being one of the last few students on campus.

I don't know why I feel such trivial memories so intensely. I wonder if college friends meet again many years later to acknowledge the elegant absurdity of having friends in college. We go through universal emotions together, at a four-year intersection, on a stage, and then we say goodbye.

There is an expiration date to all this. I don't have to tell you that none of us is permanent. We're just passing through, here and gone and then somewhere else. The world is just a rental.

I wonder if all this will be worth it one day, or if it would be better to abandon the real world and follow Jack Kerouac's road.

I have this inexplicable feeling that I am part of someone's elaborate dream, that I'm alive when they're asleep and I'm asleep when they're alive. I've always lived with this great suspicion that I don't belong here. How can you explain this feeling to anyone? You can't. There isn't a word for this feeling, so you don't tell anyone. You keep it to yourself and get used to this weird world.

You feel that you're somehow out of whack, that you took a wrong turn in the bowels of a maze and entered another world and couldn't find your way back. A maze is like that. It gets so complicated that you forget where you came from and where you were going. You stop for a moment and try to understand this little piece of the world that you occupy. And of course, you can't understand it. So, you let it go, and get used to this strange, rented world.

I imagine my old self somewhere, getting lost, meaning no harm, singing songs to feel safe. I kind of miss that guy. I wonder where he is now, and if he ever thinks of me. Maybe somewhere in this crazy dream, I'll find him again, and we'll share a laugh or two for the old times, and I'll say, "Well, look at us now." We'll walk at three in the morning and watch the sun rise over Weeks Bridge, as if, for one last time, we could relive it all again and not regret a thing.